ESSENTIAL PROSE SERIES 149

Guernica Editions Inc. acknowledges the support of the Canada Council for the Arts and the Ontario Arts Council. The Ontario Arts Council is an agency of the Government of Ontario.

We acknowledge the financial support of the Government of Canada.

eye

Marianne Micros

GUERNICA
EDITIONS
TORONTO • BUFFALO • LANCASTER (U.K.)
2018

Michael Mirolla, editor
David Moratto, Interior and cover design
Guernica Editions Inc.
1569 Heritage Way, Oakville, (ON), Canada L6M 2Z7
2250 Military Road, Tonawanda, N.Y. 14150-6000 U.S.A.
www.guernicaeditions.com

Distributors:
University of Toronto Press Distribution,
5201 Dufferin Street, Toronto (ON), Canada M3H 5T8
Gazelle Book Services, White Cross Mills
High Town, Lancaster LA1 4XS U.K.

First edition.
Printed in Canada.

Legal Deposit—Third Quarter
Library of Congress Catalog Card Number: 2017964538
Library and Archives Canada Cataloguing in Publication
Micros, Marianne, 1943-, author
Eye / Marianne Micros. -- First edition.

(Essential prose series ; 149)
Short stories.
Issued in print and electronic formats.
ISBN 978-1-77183-257-1 (softcover).--ISBN 978-1-77183-258-8 (EPUB).
--ISBN 978-1-77183-259-5 (Kindle)

I. Title. II. Series: Essential prose series ; 149

PS8576.I273E94 2018   C813'.54   C2018-900136-4   C2018-900137-2

To my mother, Alexandra (Alice),
who died in 2009 at the age of 91.
She was a natural healer,
who knew how to repel the evil eye.

Contents

No Man

THE BOY, COMING in from swimming, found a man's head in the water, caught in the sand near shore. His feet kicked into the head, and he pulled it out. The eyes, wide open and deep blue, stared at him solemnly and wisely. The boy stared back, as if hypnotized, then felt the goose pimples start crawling over his dripping body. He dug a hole in a corner of the beach, behind a rock, and buried the head, eyes downward, staring into the earth.

Frightened, the boy started to climb the steps leading up to a ruined fortress at the top. His body and shorts were drying already in the hot sun, as he walked across the cobblestones of the main street and headed upwards. He hurried past the shops and small houses, in fear that his mother would see him and call him to come do his chores.

"*Yiasou, yiasou, Panayot'*." An old toothless man hailed the boy as he ran by, old Lefteris, who had lost his mind years ago but knew everyone's name. Panayotis nodded to him abruptly. Strange images were jumping through his mind, but he couldn't sort out the colours and shapes. Then he saw Lefteris dead, lying in the middle of the street, while a donkey cart hurried off into the distance. Panayotis was frightened that such a horrible scene would come into his mind, and ran until he reached the fortress at the top of the village.

Now he could look down at what was real, the village of Molivos that climbed uphill, houses jumbled like broken puzzle pieces, the blue sea and sky joined together as one, the distant brown of the land of Turkey. The people of this island, Mytilene, or Lesbos, still considered the Turks their enemies, and every day expected an invasion. After years of domination, they could not believe they would be free forever, even now in 1937. Sometimes someone would see movement down on the shore and yell, "The Turks are coming," and everyone would go to their hideouts, hidden caves in the mountains. But these were always false alarms.

These ruins had once been a fortress against the Turks, then a fortress of the Turks, but now were mostly underground or broken apart. This was his favourite place in Molivos; he liked it better than the beach, or the fisherman's cove, because he could see so much here. Here he could dream of his future, of being a ship's captain, of owning a store, of living in Athens, or even of going to America, where the streets were paved with gold. Sometimes he came here to escape his mother's orders, or his father's bad temper, or his schoolteacher's anger when his work was not done. They were always bothering him, when all he really wanted to do was swim or sit in the fortress. This was his castle, where he was the king.

His eyes moved downward, from tier to tier of houses, down to the shore. Panayotis often played this game —trying to make his eyes travel very slowly, to hold them back from dashing to the view of the sea—but the sea always won. This time his eyes stopped, however, at the street of the marketplace, where he thought he saw a body lying in the road. And, yes, there was a donkey cart rushing off. He covered his eyes with his hand and looked again. It *was* a body and people were running toward it. Panayotis ran down the steps, down and down, until he reached the crowd. He pushed his way through and saw on the ground Lefteris' mangled body. He heard his mother shouting, "*Panayot', ella tho*, come away from there." She put him to work bringing in buckets of water and feeding the animals, as she clucked at the perverse curiosity of small boys.

The small boy, his dark eyes troubled, brought in the buckets of water and poured them into the large barrel. The little house was filled with bustle as his mother cleaned and scrubbed with his two sisters helping. While Panayotis fed the animals, the women rolled and kneaded large lumps of dough which they would take to the village oven to bake. Panayotis' father was in the mountains, milking the goats, and after that he would be working in his garden.

But the boy was hardly aware of what his family was doing. He was trying too hard to keep back the shadowy images that kept playing across his brain, to ignore the guilt and horror that had not quite come to the surface, the fear that his thoughts were murderers. Occasionally the blurred images almost came into focus, and Panayotis thought he saw this house, that his father had build with his own hands, in ruins like the castle.

"It is time to read to your grandmother," his mother called, and Panayotis washed up, dressed in his better clothes, and went next door. Old Yiayiá sat contentedly, her wrinkled hands in her lap. There were a million wrinkles on her face, and her blind eyes were tightly closed into thousands of crow's feet. She smiled when she heard her grandson enter. "Is it you, Panayot', my child?"

"Yes, Yiayiá, I am here." Panayotis picked up the torn Bible and began to read.

He read without understanding what he was saying. He felt guilty at his lack of interest in the Bible, and then another kind of guilt edged its way to the surface, making him feel twinges of fear. He stuttered over the words.

"What is the matter, my boy? Something is not right with you, I can tell. Tell your Yiayiá all about it, your Yiayiá who loves you so much."

"I am afraid, Yiayiá, of losing you someday, you are so old." It was true, he could see her in his mind, stretched out in her coffin, in her good black dress, and people throwing flowers on her.

"Ach, Panayot'. We must all die someday. And I will be ready to join my Yiannis, and the other Panayotis, your uncle, when the time comes. You must not miss me, but grow up to be a fine man, like your father and his brothers. Now help me to my bed, I am tired."

Panayotis let her lean on him, then covered her and kissed her on the cheek. She smiled at him from her pillow.

Panayotis was so quiet for the rest of the day that his mother kept feeling his head to see if he had a fever. Finally it was bedtime and Panayotis fell asleep in spite of his spinning thoughts, hoping that the next day would be better.

But when he awoke the next morning, his mother came in to tell him that his grandmother had died in the night.

Panayotis dashed from the room, crashing into his father as he tried to run outside. "Stop, boy," his father yelled. "She was very old. We all must die sometime."

He ran past his sisters, who were quietly weeping in the courtyard, and into his grandmother's house to see if it were true. She was lying peacefully on her bed, with lighted candles flickering around her, and three mourners sitting by the bed, weeping and mumbling. "I have done this," he thought. "But I didn't want to. I didn't want her to die."

He could not face his family. Although he still wore his pyjamas, he ran and ran, out of the village, out into the country, stumbling on the large rocks. He slowed down to a walk then, and walked for two hours, until he found a hiding place in a chasm which had been caused by an earthquake.

"Wake up, Yiayiá," he cried loudly to the air. "Come back to life. Please." He lay down and cried until he fell asleep.

When he woke up, it was already afternoon, and he felt pangs of hunger. As if in answer to a call, a goat's bell tinkled not far away. Panayotis crawled silently to the place where he had heard the bell, hid, then pounced on a runaway goat, ready to be milked. He chased after the frightened animal, caught her, and squirted milk into his mouth. He was still hungry, but the milk helped, and he let the goat go. She jumped away, then stopped, and settled herself at a short distance from Panayotis, staring at him cautiously, as if she were making sure that he would not run away from her.

Visions started to jump through the boy's head again, and, in order to stop them, he walked around, picking up stones. After he had accumulated a pile of stones, he began making a circle out of them, building a ring of protection for himself. He pretended he was building a house, a castle maybe, or a fortress, but he couldn't pile the stones very high without their falling down. He climbed out of the chasm to see if anyone was coming, but saw no one, and slipped back down into his hiding place.

He thought of his grandmother and how she had encouraged him to read and to go to school. He remembered the old stories she used to tell him—especially the one about the man who had put out the eye of a giant and had told the giant his name was "no man." When the giant was asked who had done this to him, he had replied, "No man did it." Panayotis thought that perhaps he should call himself "no man." He would build his own castle, high on a mountaintop, and tell everyone that no man lived there. He could then be alone.

He thought of what his family would be doing now. They would be crying over his grandmother's body, praying in the candlelight, and guarding her so that no evil spirits would hurt her. If a cat jumped over her body, she would not decay, and her dead body would arise and walk at night. That would not be so bad; he could talk to her then. Panayotis considered taking a cat into the room. Then he began to cry again, and cried himself to sleep.

It was dark when he awoke, and he heard shouting in the distance. He crouched down behind the rocks, hoping the searchers would not see him. They came closer and closer. "Panayot'. Panayot'." His mother was there; he could hear her crying. He couldn't stand the crying and shouted, "Mamá. Babá." His father lifted him up in his arms, crying too, and the party joyfully headed home, followed by the lost goat.

When he was in his room, warm and fed, and the other children asleep, his mother asked him why he had run away. "We are all sorry that Yiayiá has died, but we do not run away."

"I am a murderer. My thoughts are murderers." He told his parents of the visions, of what he had seen. "And I see them all the time," he added. "Right now Mrs. Papagiani is ready to have her baby, and she will have a girl by tomorrow morning."

His mother shrieked. "Yes! She is ready to have her baby. I saw her husband tonight, and he said any time now."

"Perhaps he has the evil eye," she whispered.

"Little boys do not have the evil eye," his father yelled angrily, "but they do receive the evil eye. Someone has put the eye upon him, in jealousy of his good looks and intelligence."

His mother brought a glass of water and put three drops of oil into it. The oil dispersed. "He does not have the eye," she said. "But to be sure I will take him to Kyria Ourania tomorrow morning. Whatever is wrong, she will heal him. You go to sleep now, *poulaki*." She pinched her son's cheek. "And do not worry. I am sure you are no murderer. You loved your Yiayiá. You would not hurt a fly."

She left, making the sign of the cross three times. His father patted him, then followed her.

In the morning, after his milk, Panayotis was cleaned and dressed and brushed, and he and his mother set off for Kyria Ourania's hut, which was up high near the fortress. Her house was filled with chickens and the smell of herbs. Kyria Ourania was stirring an odd-smelling mixture in a pot over the fire.

"*Kalimera.* And what can I do for you? Is the boy sick?"

The old lady sat down with them. She wore bright colours, unlike other old women, and a white bandanna over her grey hair. While Panayotis' mother told her the story, Kyria Ourania clucked and grunted and shook her head.

"Perhaps the boy has a gift," she concluded. "Perhaps you will take my place, boy," she said, a bit threateningly. "I cannot see as much as you have seen. And, by the way, Mrs. Papagiani had a fine baby girl at 3 o'clock this morning." Kyria Ourania gurgled in her throat and smacked her lips.

"Do you hurt anyplace?" she asked.

Panayotis shook his head.

"Lie down. I will try a charm, but I cannot promise it will help."

The old lady made the sign of the cross all over the boy's head and body with a swab dipped in oil, herbs, and dung, and chanted a spell three times. Then she chanted two other spells three times each.

"When did you start seeing these things?"

"It started when I found the head."

"The head, Panayoti, what do you mean the head?" Both women were shouting at him.

"I found the head of a man in the water. It stared at me. Then I started seeing things."

Kyria Ourania waved her arms in the air. "Where is it? Where is it now? This cannot be."

"I buried it."

"Quickly. Take us there."

The three ran off so quickly that they attracted a crowd of people yelling, "*Pou pate, pou pate.*" But they were in too much of a hurry to explain. When they arrived at the beach, half the village was behind them. Panayotis led them to the place where he had buried the head and dug it up for them. There it was, eyes downward.

"Wait, no, wait," Kyria Ourania yelled, but Panayotis had already turned the head around. The blue eyes stared out at the gathered crowd.

"Do not look at it," she cried. "Please, do not look. It is the head of Orpheus. It will make you see the future. It will show you things you do not want to know."

But her words came too late. Many people had seen

9

the eyes. The road was full of babbling people, wandering in circles. Panayotis knew they must all be seeing the same visions he was having. He saw foreign soldiers, not the Turks this time, with guns, capturing and destroying his country, laying waste the land, bringing starvation, death by famine. The people went home to weep and to wonder, to try to prepare for the future. Panayotis quietly climbed up the hill. He left the head lying on the beach, staring upwards.

The fortress stood as it had for centuries, and as it would for centuries more, broken apart, parts missing, but still there on the hill, enduring everything.

The Sacrifice

i. *Miracle*

I CLUTCH MY baby to me as I walk to the church, the church where the miracles happen, where people are cured, the blind see, the crippled throw away their canes and walk. I grew up in a world of miracles, on my island of Tinos, and now I have had a miracle happen to me. I could not get pregnant for twelve years, and now I have a baby girl. *Panayia*, the Virgin Maria, has answered my prayers. Now it is time to bring the baby to the Virgin, and my mother-in-law, my *pethera*, hurries me along. I must do as I vowed, throw my baby from the bell tower of the church, and, if my faith is strong, the *Panayia* will not let the baby be harmed. Many women do this; the baby lives if the mother has faith, but dies if the mother hesitates. I do not want to take the chance now. I have waited too long for this child, and I do not believe that the *Panayia* would want me to sacrifice the baby. She was also a mother. Would she have thrown her son away? I do not think so.

As we draw near the church, I stop. My *pethera* prods me. "What are you doing? Do not lose faith. See what the *Panayia* has done for you." I cannot go in, I start to scream and hold my baby, I must save the child, I will not throw her from the tower. My *pethera* begins to cry and moan, begging me to continue. "It will be bad luck if you don't. It will be bad luck for us all, the whole family."

I start to run away. Suddenly I hear an evil, adult giggle from my baby's mouth. I look at the child in my arms and see only a large, wriggling snake. I drop it and scream, start to faint. It is the *stringlos*, the evil demon who takes the shape of a baby. I will die now. But the priest is there, he utters the protective chant, and I say it with him. I live.

But where is my baby? Where is my baby? I get up and start to run, a crowd of people following me. When I reach the house, I hear a cry. She is in there, she is all right, only hungry. I lock the door against the crowd, even against my mother-in-law, and put the baby to my breast. I am relieved. The *Panayia* does not want my baby after all.

My *pethera* bangs on the door and shouts, "We must hurry to the church."

"No, no, she does not want the baby."

"Oh, yes, she does. An evil demon tried to prevent it, to tempt you. We must go now, and hurry."

"Soon," I say. "Soon."

I rock the baby and croon lullabies.

I wake up. How long have I been sleeping? The baby! The baby is gone. "*Pethera! Pethera!*" She is gone, too.

I run, pushing through the crowds, trying to reach the bell tower in time. I push aside mothers and babies, and just as I reach the tower, I see something falling from above, it is falling on me. I hold out my arms, and my little daughter drops into them and looks at me, comforted. I hold her to me and the tears stream down my face. It is a miracle. She is saved. When *Pethera* reaches me, she is appeased. The baby is saved, the *Panayia* has made this happen. We walk home, slowly now, surrounded by people crossing themselves. I turn my back as another baby falls down, to the stones this time. I do not look to see if he is alive.

When we arrive home, I hurry to my icon of *Panayia* to give thanks. She looks at me with sadness, her eyes filled with tears.

ii. *The Curse*

I was named Maria for the Virgin, who made my birth possible. My mother had promised me to the Virgin, but when my grandmother threw me from the bell tower of the church as vowed, I fell into my mother's waiting arms. This was called a miracle.

I have to get away from this island, this family, these people who believe in such terrible things, and who would throw a baby from a tower. The church is filled with gold, silver, precious jewels, while people on the streets starve. The priests are rich and fat, while we go hungry. The Virgin has such treasures; she does not need someone's baby. I will do anything to leave all this. If my mother were here, perhaps it would be better, but she died soon after the miracle.

One evening I see a man watching me, a man of about forty. He follows me. I am frightened, but curious. He talks to me. He says he knows I am unhappy here, and he will marry me and take me away, to a place where there is no church of the *Panayia*, no miracles. I say yes.

My husband is an odd man. I only see him at night. In the morning he is gone, sometimes he is missing for days. But he is kind to me, and we now have two fine children. We live on a small island with few inhabitants, and I do not have to follow superstitions.

One day two strangers come to my door, a woman dressed in black and a priest. They ask me about my husband. The woman has a picture of him. She says, "He was my husband, too. Some people here recognized him and sent for me." I am frightened, for myself and for my children. "I didn't know. I didn't know."

"He died four years ago," the woman whispers.

I do not believe it, but the priest says that we will find out. He will hide, and when my husband comes in at night, he will perform the ceremony that puts the living dead to sleep.

My husband comes. He is afraid. The priest quickly chants and throws oil on him. My husband disappears. Now I am alone ... except for my children. But when I go to their beds, they are gone, only their rumpled clothes remain.

I curse the Virgin Maria for saving my life.

iii. *The Return*

I live alone in a tiny hut on the side of a mountain on the island of Tinos. There is no smooth place left on my skin. I can feel the wrinkles whirling around each other, the indentations pocking my face. But I do not own a mirror, it would be bad luck.

Every day I gather herbs and mix them with sheep's dung, oils, and animal flesh. People come to me for cures, and I sell them my mixtures and chant for them. As a widow who was never really married, a mother of children who were never really born, this is the only way I can make a living.

Sometimes when I see a happy woman with a fine husband and happy children frisking about her skirts, I cast the evil eye on the children. They become very ill, and when the mother comes to me for a cure, I tell her that I have lost my power for the day.

I do not go to church, and I keep no icons. The curse of the Virgin Maria has been on me since my birth. I despise her for allowing me to live. Every morning when I wake up alive, I curse the *Panayia*.

One day, while seeking herbs, I see something partially buried in the dirt. I dig it out, and it is an icon—the *Panayia* holding her child sadly, a tear stained with dirt resting on her cheek. I bury again the face that I detest so much and return home.

The next day I try to stay inside my house. My feet itch and my hands burn until I go out, and I am drawn to that spot, where I must dig up the Virgin again. The tear is still on her face, and she seems to accuse me. "Why do you hate me so much?" I say to her. "What do you want from me now?"

I take the icon home with me, place it near my herbs and foul-smelling mixtures, and talk to her. Every day and night now I complain to her and curse her.

One night something wakes me up. Something inside my brain is talking to me. I sit up. The icon is lighted up, and I go to it. The Virgin is crying. "My baby is dead," she seems to be saying as she holds the infant. "Why are you alive? You who curse me day and night."

"I lost my children, too," I scream at her.

"Your children were never alive."

I know now that I was not meant to live. It was an accident that my mother caught me that day. It was not a miracle at all.

"I am sorry," I say and leave the house. I walk to the tower. I climb the steps, slowly, one at a time. I reach the top and look down at the hard pavement, then out at the sky. Gleams of light are just beginning to streak across the darkness. I jump, fall quickly, smash on the cobblestone.

As I walk away from my broken body, I see a woman holding a baby; she bends over my body, crying. As she turns away from the body and looks at me, I see that she is the *Panayia* of my icon. She is crying for me. "Poor Maria," she mutters and shakes her head, clutching her baby tightly, as if she is afraid she will lose him.

I walk away, feeling her sad eyes following me forever.

The Midwife

Monday, 2:00 a.m.

SHE COMES EVERY morning at this time and sits beside my bed. She talks and talks but I cannot understand her. Only a few words now and then. *Goat. Chicken. Lemons. Basil. Sunshine. Babies.* Sometimes she cries. I lie there listening while she mumbles. She is a shadow in the darkness, dressed in black, telling her incomprehensible stories.

My mother. Dead for twenty years. Forever present in my darkness. Sometimes giving me advice.

Chamomile, she now says. *Hamomee-lee.* And then she says, *Horta.*

Chamomile tea helps with labour pains, as does the juice from boiled greens. Greece is a country with little grass, but the mountain greens bring strength to the ill —and to pregnant women.

I am not surprised when a young man knocks on my door and calls through my window. "Fotini. Come. My wife is in labour. She is suffering. Please help us. Bring our baby into the world for us."

I change into a loose housedress, one that had belonged to my mother, slip on sandals, gather up chamomile, some dandelion greens, and other herbs, and follow him to his house. As we draw near, I can hear his wife screaming. I quickly enter. "It will be all right," I say. I touch her stomach and look into her eyes. "The baby will be here soon." I start water boiling for the tea and also for the greens. I feed her the broth from the greens and help her sip the tea. Then I encourage her to push. The time has come. The baby boy comes out into the world. He is beautiful.

"Thank you, Fotini," the man says, and his wife smiles down at her baby.

My eyes water. I am happy for them. But I remember my own baby, a sweet girl I named Eftihia, happiness. Because I was seventeen and unmarried, my mother took the baby to the priest, who gave her to a couple in another village. I had loved the baby's father, but he had gone away soon after I became pregnant. I never heard from him again. I never saw my daughter again. She would be thirty years old now. Once, years ago, I walked to the village where I thought she lived, but my mother and the priest followed me and brought me home. "She is happy. She is with a good family. Do not disturb her life."

So I did not.

I learned my mother's trade—midwifery, healing, repelling the evil eye, performing rituals for good luck and success. "No one will ever want to marry you," my mother said, and she had been correct. In this small village an unwed mother was a curse on everyone. I was considered unclean. Except when it came to helping others with their troubles.

Tuesday, 2:00 a.m.

Eftihia, my mother says. Happiness. She is giggling in the darkness. Then she growls and swats me with her slipper. I feel nothing. She must be frustrated that she cannot hurt me with her blows. I am responsible for ruining her life and her reputation—at least she thinks so. She herself had no husband, though she claimed that she was married, that my father left her for a *putana* who lived in the wilderness high up on the mountain. But I never met him. No one knew who he was. I was always Alexandra's daughter. If I asked people if they had known my father, they never answered. Perhaps the devil was my father. I make the sign of the cross three times as I lie here.

Later that morning a woman comes to me. Her seven-year-old son is very ill. I follow her home. He is screaming and writhing. I can tell this was caused by the evil eye. I take a glass of water and drop oil in it. The oil sinks to the bottom of the glass. It is the *mati*, I say, the eye. I say the words that I learned from my mother and make the sign of the cross on the boy's forehead. Then I say the prayer I learned from my grandmother. He is quiet now. Tomorrow he will be well again.

Wednesday, 2:00 a.m.

My mother is crying. I can almost feel wet tears dropping on my face. Her mouth is moving rapidly but the language sounds like gibberish. *Koritsaki*, she says. Little girl. She keeps speaking but I try to tune her out, to sleep. She shrieks out my name. After a while, she disappears, and I finally fall asleep. I wake at dawn with the crow of the rooster. My mother is gone.

A boy hands a letter through the window. A letter from the next village. My heart is thumping. Perhaps this is from Eftihia. All that is in the envelope is a small amulet, an evil eye protector worn by a child.

Thursday, 2:00 a.m.

I am dreaming that I am holding my baby girl. I feel such joy. This is truly happiness. When I wake up and know it is not true, I begin to tremble. My mother's hand is on my arm. She is smiling. *Avgo*, she says. Egg.

Today is like all the others. I get eggs from my chickens. I milk my goat. I work in my garden. When customers come, I give them whatever concoction will be helpful to them. My neighbour Kalliope tells me that her mother is dying, is suffering. I give her herbs that will ease the pain. I remember my mother's final illness. I asked her where my daughter was, what happened to my lover Yiannis. She opened her mouth but no words came out.

Now she cannot stop talking. Sometimes she keeps me awake all night. Words I do not understand.

Friday, 2:00 a.m.

There is a man with my mother—younger than she is, about my age. He pats her shoulder. He looks at me loving-ly. I recognize him. Yiannis. I sit up, reach out for him, but my hand goes through him. "You are dead. Yianni, I missed you so. And now we will never be together, at least not in life." He smiles sadly. He nods. "Where is our daughter?" I ask him. He looks troubled. I see that he does not know. He does not speak but stands there nodding at my mother's unending cascade of words. I leave my bed and make myself a coffee. I see them stand-ing beside my bed—as if I am still there. "Look at me," I cry. "I am over here." My mother continues to talk to the bed, but Yiannis turns and looks at me. He walks away, through the closed door, into the darkness. *Skotathi*, she says. Darkness.

I hear the news that afternoon that Yiannis has died. He had been living in America all these years. He never married. I get out my mother's black dress and veil, the clothing of a widow, and put them on.

Saturday, 2:00 a.m.

She is angry today, her mouth moving frantically, her hands gesturing. I want to grab her words, throw them back at her. Perhaps she is still angry at me. "Mother," I say, "I have carried on your work, lived forever in this tiny house. I loved Yiannis, but you stole my daughter. I can never forgive you. I am the one with the right to

21

be angry. Not you." I turn my back and stare at the wall. But I can see her shadow on the wall, her hands waving wildly, her mouth uttering curses or threats. All I understand is my name. *Fotini.*

I go to the fireplace where my herbs are drying. I take some, mix them together, boil them. Then I pour the mixture into a cup. I hold it up, as if toasting my mother. "Mother, I repel you, once and for all. Leave me now. Go to the land of the dead. I avert your curse. Take it off me."

I had tried this before, without success, but I feel that this time it might work. My mother turns and looks at me. Her mouth grows still. She is silent. She holds out her hands as if in supplication. As if asking for forgiveness. I cannot forgive her. But perhaps I can make her talk, put my hand behind her back, find a mechanical gadget, and move her mouth. I will say the words I want to hear from her. I am sorry. I love you. I love Eftihia. Go find her.

Sunday, 5:00 a.m.

My mother did not come this morning. I slept well until now. Now I drink my coffee, dress in my widow's clothing, and pack a lunch. The evil eye amulet is hanging on a string around my neck. I am walking to the village where I believe that Eftihia was taken. What will I do if she has had a child out of wedlock? Will I let her keep her baby? Will I forgive her? I will climb the mountain and walk the dirt paths until I find her. I will sit by her bed and hold her hand. I will speak clearly and slowly. Not gibberish. Words with meaning. Words that I hope she will hear and understand.

Eftihia.

Thirteen

i. *Virgin Mother*

I SIT IN the ashes of the hearth, staring at the large black pot swinging from its peg, listening to the boiling of the soup. Occasionally I stir the strong-smelling mixture, my arm circling in the same motion I have seen my mother make.

I have no father. My mother says that she has known no man. She always smiles when she tells me this, her few teeth gleaming. She is immaculate, she says, just like the one she was named for, Maria, and that is why she named me Christiana. I am a child of God, sister of Christ. I used to pray hopefully to my Brother to come visit me. He never did. And I wondered if my mother had been joking.

Last week, after my thirteenth birthday, my friend Toula from the village whispered to me, "Who is your father? Babies cannot be born without the help of men. My mother says Lefteris is your father."

I'm sure that is not possible. Lefteris often smiles at me, but only as he smiles at everyone. He can only smile

—emptily, innocently—as he walks the cobblestones begging for food and drink and announcing the end of the world. "It is coming, it is coming," he cries daily. "Pray that you will be saved. Line up, good people, at my right hand. Come to my left, evil ones, and I'll push you to Hell." If someone gives him food, he blesses that person: "You are saved."

Is this my God, author of my immaculate conception? I seek out my reflection in the well. Is there emptiness in the eyes, a flaccid openness of the mouth? Not yet, but there is a look of him, something I don't understand, a look of never having been touched.

Mamá is unhappy this week. Someone has stolen her icon.

"My friend is gone," she says, weeping—her friend, the Virgin, with whom she converses almost unceasingly. "Who would do such a thing?"

Yesterday she ran all over the village yelling about her loss. People came to their windows, but only shrugged their shoulders. They do not love my mother, but they respect, even fear her somewhat. Without her help, many of them would die of disease or of evil spells. They are polite to her, so that she will not curse them. But no one knew anything about her icon.

Mamá is mysterious today. This morning she stretched a cloth across two sticks and tried to draw the Virgin with coal, until, frustrated, she threw her picture into the fire. She sketched faces over and over in the dirt of our floor, then rubbed them out.

"I must have her," she cried.

She runs into the house now, grabs me, and shakes me by the shoulders. "Christiana. You. You must do it. Only a virgin ... you are a virgin, are you not?

"Yes, Mamá, of course." I am shaking.

"Here." She gives me a pen, a pot of ink, and a tablet of paper. I stare. I have never seen anything like this before.

"Where did you find these, Mamá?"

She smiles. "Never mind. Draw me the Virgin. For me, my love."

I turn the pen around, confused, until she puts my fingers around it and helps me make my first mark. I make another, then another. I look at the black pot hanging over the fire and copy its form.

"That is a pot, not my Virgin. That pot is not a Virgin, it has been heated many times."

"I must practise on something first, something from our household. The Virgin is so pure—what if I smudge her?"

So I practise. I draw our hut, its inside and outside. I draw the clouds in the sky, the cypress tree, my reflection in the well. I feel music and light come through my fingers. But how can I make the Virgin?

"Why must I do this, Mamá?"

"She is needed. Aleko has asked me to save his wife and baby. The baby cannot come out, and they will both soon die. I must have my *Panayia* to help me. Try, my child, try."

I draw all night, while my mother coaxes. After the sun comes up and the rooster crows, Mamá goes out to the well for a moment—the Virgin leaps from my fingers onto the paper.

"Here she is, Mamá."

She takes the drawing and runs to Aleko's house.

I wait for two hours, then walk down to the village. Through the window I see Aleko's wife in bed—sleeping, I think, not dead. There is a cradle next to her. Yes, the child is breathing. In the corner is an icon—a real icon—the Virgin smiles.

My mother comes out now.

"You didn't need my drawing," I say. "They have an icon."

"No," she smiles, "that is yours, you made it."

"But look!" I point inside.

"I know. Magic. The magic of Christ. Christiana."

I don't understand, but I say nothing. We go home, to eat and to make medicines for tomorrow's callers. We go to bed, but I cannot sleep. A shadow at my window frightens me.

"Maria."

"No, it is me—Christiana."

Lefteris puts his head inside the window. He lowers inside the bag he carries everyplace, reaches down to open it.

"I am sorry that I borrowed your mother's icon. I wanted her to worry a little." I can see his eyes shine in the moonlight, his teeth sparkle, and he winks. "Here you are. Goodbye."

I am holding an icon. I light the candle to see it better —it feels too light. I am looking at my drawing of a smiling Virgin. She smiles at me. I quietly put her on the table. In the morning, will the Virgin be made of blue ink on paper, or of bright paints in a frame? I take my pen and paper and draw a baby wrapped in a warm blanket. It looks like Aleko's baby. It also looks like the baby I will have someday. I see that it is my baby. I place the drawing on the table next to the Virgin. I smile contentedly in my sleep, for I am untouched.

ii. *The Same Thing*

Christy's birthday it was Christy's birthday her thirteenth lucky unlucky thirteen and she whipped round and round on the tilt-a-whirl her eyes shut tight her head leaning on the shoulder of the dark-haired boy. He was eighteen and wanted to whirl with her. She was happy little chills ran through her new body she was tall and curvy. She could hear Elvis Presley's voice— "ooo—ooo —ooo—ooo—ooo—ooo—I'm all shook up," and imagined his swively body.

The ride stopped and he wanted to take her home. But her mother was there waiting for her. "No. He's too old for you. Don't you know what he's after? They all want the same thing." She grabbed Christy's arm and walked her home.

Christy dreamed about the dark-haired boy for nights, but he ignored her in school and was always holding hands with a blonde girl whom people said was "easy." Then he was killed in a car crash. She cried in bed that night and then forgot him.

"I want to be a writer," she thought. She always said that to herself when she was depressed. She tried to see life as a writer would and searched for metaphors. "Life is a rainbow with a pot of gold at the end," or "Life is like a tilt-a-whirl, with twists and turns, threatening to cut your head off but only making you throw up" or "Life is a poem that ends in a couple of gasps" or "Life is a comedy and God a stand-up comic who sometimes muffs his lines."

She hadn't thought about writing in a long time only about boys their smooth hips and long legs. Her body felt nice. But her mother wouldn't let her go to parties or dances or movies with boys.

"I wish I had a father." Her father had died in the War, and all she knew of him was from the glazed-eyed picture on the piano. Her mother hardly talked to men now, and almost every day she would say to Christy, "They're all after the same thing."

Christy wrote down a dream she had had once. Her mother was the Virgin Mary and she was the baby Jesus crying in her lap.

Mama you are too pure you are too clean.

Then her mother turned into a lascivious whore a slut dressed in red, winking.

no mother no   where is my father
you have no father child   only God
so far away so bodiless

sex my child is like a cooking pot the more you are heated the blacker you get

One day a strange man came to the door. Oh where had she seen him before his dark eyes his black hair. Her mother knew him, but wouldn't let him in. He came back again and again, wanting to see Christy, until he was allowed to step inside, smile, and pat Christy's head.

"Who *is* he?"

"An old friend."

"But who?"

She began to see him in the restaurant where she and her friends had Cokes after school. He was waiting until she was alone.

"Hi, Christy. I've missed you, you know."

"Who *are* you?"

"Hasn't she told you yet? Oh, for heaven's sake. I'm your dad."

"No, you're not. You can't be. My Dad was killed in the War. He's dead. Dead as a doornail. Dead as a tor-pedoed rat. Or are you his ghost?"

"That was your mother's husband. He died before you were even conceived. She should have told you. You're old enough now."

Christy ran home. He couldn't be her father he wore ragged old clothes stained with paint had holes in his jeans he was an artist or something. She looked in the mirror. Did she look like him? The image blurred on her she could never see what she really looked like if only she could be someone else looking at her.

Her mother had to tell her the truth now. "I was an

evil woman, Christy, and I deserve to be punished. I wouldn't blame you if you hated me. But I want to make you into a better woman than I am. You don't help me any, the way you shake your hips when you walk."

A story jumped out at Christy, a story about a pure woman who decided never to have relations with men, but one day she found a baby in her bed and a note that said, "Happy Birthday. Love, God." Christy wrote it all down, describing the baby in great detail until she could see it, almost feel it in her arms.

"You are my own child," she said to the story, "my own forever. And you will never hurt me."

iii. *Times Three*

I have turned thirteen many times; thousands of years ago, or a long way inside myself, is an image of thirteen that has been repeated time after time, perhaps person after person. The face looks into a well, a mirror, or another face, and says, "Is that I?" and then "That is I."

Now I am three times thirteen and my daughter is thirteen. She blows out the candles all at once and yells, "I'm a teenager!" She jumps and dances around the room.

I help her brush her hair and we look in the mirror at ourselves and each other. Her hair is lighter than mine, her face fuller, her eyes less black. For once, there is no petulance to the shape of her lips, no gloom in her eyes. She will always be shorter than I am—that's good. But I was once she. She will be I.

I know that tonight she will tease her boyfriend until he kisses her. I know that she will slap him when he tries to touch her slightly below the breast. I know that she will defiantly come home one-half hour late, because she will wait outside for that long before she comes in. Then she will smile and say, "Don't worry. I'm a big girl now." Or her eyes will say it.

But there are many things I don't know. I don't know what kind of mother I have been, what kind of mother she will be, what I have made her into. I have tried to be the opposite of what my mother was. I have never said "Sex is dirty" or "Men are no good." I *have* called sex "dangerous" and men "over-anxious." I often say, "Come home early" or "Be careful." I am nervous about tonight, her first date. She is only thirteen.

"Well, have fun. Be ... have a good time. Come home at 11 o'clock."

"Sure, Mom."

Then she hugs me. "I love you, Mom."

The doorbell rings.

"Are you going to be alone tonight, Ma? No dates?"

"No."

"Heck. We'll stay here with you and watch TV."

She clutches my hand. She is perspiring.

"Get out of here!" I stick out my tongue and nudge her, until she runs to the door.

In the mirror I see myself at thirteen — a face vulnerable, shy, pretty but unformed — and over it another face — older, somewhat creased, heavier, more interesting. I take out my sketch pad and draw us blurred together, two people—no three—my daughter is here, too, and countless other girl-women.

I tack the picture up on the wall of my studio and walk through the house, a house of many doors and windows, of many mirrors. My own house. A house belonging to the woman in my sketch, the many myselves, and to my daughter in all her ages. It is not a house for men. Widowed, never again married, I don't expect that a man will ever live here permanently. My daughter's stay is temporary, too. When will she leave? How long will I be here?

But tonight I am thirteen again, changing, turning, growing, looking at my newly-developed self ... until she comes in the door, flushing and breathless. I go out and another comes in. We wait for our next thirteenth birthday.

Eye

A MAN WAS hanging from a tree, swinging back and forth, in the very place where animals are butchered. His head dangled, casting a strange oblong shadow that moved rhythmically as his body swayed. He was dressed in dirty work pants and a rumpled white T-shirt. His eyes were bulging out, his mouth swollen. The noon sun was burning his skin. The rope was tight around his neck but not so tight that it had caused his death. It was Stavros Yorgopoulos, the mayor of our village. An overturned chair underneath gave the appearance of suicide — but I did not think so.

His wife Chrysoula had collapsed at his feet. She had grasped his one foot and was trying to pull him down, but her weakened state, as she lay in a half-faint on the ground, made that impossible.

Three men came with knives to cut him down. As they struggled with the body, I led Chrysoula back to her house. When Stavros was brought home, I would help her wash and dress him. That was one of the jobs I held in the village — to prevent death when possible, to prepare the dead for burial, to comfort the living. Now I made tea for Chrysoula while we waited, but she continued to wail and cry, not even looking at the cup I placed before her. We had moved the table to one side and placed a cot in the middle of the room. I had filled some pails with water and brought some strips of cloth for washing the body.

After the body had been carried in and laid on the cot, I inspected his neck. I could see that someone's fingers had made the dark bruises. It was not the rope that had killed him.

"He did not commit suicide," Chrysoula said. "He was a happy man."

"You are right. Someone choked him to death."

"Help me, Katina," Chrysoula cried. "Find out who did this."

People in the village frequently asked me, a middle-aged lady, unmarried, with no children, for help. I was known to do magic with my herbs, my potions, my touch, my words. People in Athens were starting to laugh at such things — but not here. I was all the villagers had to keep the darkness away. They did not know that the darkness is always there — that darkness can even be comforting.

I had many clients, mostly women, who came for help — with love, with childbirth, with ending a pregnancy, with repelling the evil eye or blocking a curse. Sometimes people wanted me to cause harm to others — but I always refused. Men visited me, too, hoping for success or money. I would not guarantee the results. A few people asked me to contact the dead. Though I had had experiences seeing the dead, I could not force them to come to me or to speak through me.

Many people asked me to heal physical and emotional illnesses. Kyria Mavropoulou brought her six-month-old baby to my door. I had noticed him many times—a healthy, chubby boy, always laughing and holding his arms out, even to strangers. But now he looked flushed and tired. There were dark circles under his eyes, and he was shaking, but was not fevered. There seemed to be no reason for his sickness. He also was yawning repeatedly. Right away, I recognized the symptoms of the *mati*, the evil eye. I asked Kyria if anyone had recently admired her baby. She, of course, said that everyone did—but I asked her if anyone in particular had exclaimed about the child's beauty.

"There was the foreign girl, the *xeni*," she said. "She is visiting the Yorgopoulos family. She said he was beautiful and even held him."

I thought this was likely the source of the illness. People could give the evil eye without even meaning to. I took a glass of water and dropped olive oil into it. The oil fell to the bottom. Now I knew that this was the evil eye. I made the sign of the cross three times and spat three times into the air. I gave Kyria Mavropoulou some medicine that I had spooned into a small bag, mostly to appease her, but I knew that I had to do more than that.

It was noon now and the sun very hot. I washed my face and hands and changed into my church dress. I wanted to look good when I met the foreigner. She wouldn't be afraid of me, the way some of the villagers were. She surely wouldn't believe in the powers of healing and magic. I had my medal of the Virgin Mary around my neck. I touched it for luck.

The stones were sharp along the path as I walked to the Yorgopoulos home. I needed new shoes. Perhaps the *xeni* would pay me to get her out of this trouble. Soon word would spread that a foreigner might have caused a baby's sickness. I did not want the villagers to take action. I must do something first. I walked around the chickens strutting down the dirt path and looked down to watch for donkey droppings and to avoid the sun's rays. The young woman was sitting out front in a chair, basking in the hot sun. I wanted to tell her that this was the most dangerous time of day—but I did not.

She smiled when she saw me approach and spoke to me in hesitant Greek. "*Yiasou*," she said. I spoke to her slowly. She understood me quite well. Her parents had always spoken Greek to her in Canada, she said. She said that in Canada people called her Mary but that I could call her by her Greek name, Maria. I asked her about herself—she was a university student on holiday, seeking information about her background. "I believe Kyria Yorgopoulou is my cousin," she said excitedly. "She has told me to call her Aunt Chrysoula."

She offered me a chair and went inside to drag one out. I was relieved that the family was not at home. They would probably not want me sitting in the open, right in front of their house, though they had come to me often when they needed something. In fact, Chrysoula had used my love spell to win her husband, Stavros, to take him away from the promiscuous Soula.

Now I sat and spoke in a friendly way with Maria. She did not have a boyfriend, she told me, though she liked one of her fellow students very much. But he thought of her only as a friend. They studied together. If only he would just look at her!

"Oh, I think he will do that soon," I said. "I have a feeling about that."

"Do you get intuitions? I sometimes do, too. I just feel that this man is the one for me."

"Yes," I said, nodding. For a moment, I worried that Maria would be my rival in the arts that I knew so well.

Maria offered me some cold water. When she came back with two glasses, I looked her in the eye. She began to yawn. How could I explain? I decided on the direct approach. "Have you heard of the evil eye?"

"My mother is superstitious about that, but I never believed it really," she answered.

"You need now to believe."

I told her the truth, about the baby and the *mati*. Maria was horrified. She said that she would never hurt a child, that she wanted children herself and loved them.

"Please, Maria, we must go to Kyria Mavropoulou's house and tell her that her baby is not so beautiful after all. That will surely work. But first I will pray with you."

We held hands and closed our eyes. I said the prayer silently to myself. The prayer passed on from woman to woman throughout the generations must never be revealed to strangers. I crossed myself three times, and Mary did the same.

She and I walked to the Mavropoulos house and knocked on the door. When she opened the door, Kyria Mavropoulou looked angry and frightened. I passed her and went directly to the baby's cradle. He was so still that I was frightened. His mother rushed to him, blocking Maria's way. "It is all right," I told her. "We are here to reverse the spell."

Maria called out, "Your baby is not so beautiful. He is just average, not even average." We spat into the air three times, as I prayed. Then we left.

Kyria Mavropoulou knocked on my door the next day, holding her smiling and healthy baby. "Thank you," she said. "And thank you to the foreign girl."

I went to see Maria then, carrying a little packet, one with a love potion. "This is for the boy you like," I told her. "Thank you," she said, smiling. "Is the baby okay?"

"Yes, he is perfect."

"I will come back with my new husband and my own baby someday. I will come to see you."

That night I dreamed that Maria and her baby came back to the village. They were both dressed in blue. Her husband had died, she told me, in a car accident. She would live here with me now. And when I died, she would carry on my business.

I went to warn her, but she was gone. Chrysoula gave me her address and I wrote, but the letter came back to me, with a note that she was no longer at that address. She had left a photograph of herself standing in front of the

Yorgopoulos house. "Would you like this?" Chrysoula asked me.

I took the picture and placed it on the small table just below my icon of the Virgin. Every day I mix my herbs, waiting for Maria to return. Every day—but today is different. I have been asked to investigate a suspicious death.

Chrysoula and I slowly took off Stavros's shirt and pants. She motioned for me to stand back while she pulled down the underpants that were digging into his flesh and gently moved them down his legs and feet. Together we washed him, Chrysoula sobbing as her hand moved softly across his flesh. We dressed him in the suit he wore to church and combed his hair.

One of Chrysoula's cousins sat with Stavros when we went to the village telephone to call Australia, where Stavros and Chrysoula's son lived. Alexander had already left for Greece, his wife told Chrysoula. He was going to surprise them, was planning to buy a house there to live in during the summers and rent out at other times. He had heard, no doubt, that tourism was growing, that foreigners would come to this small village so close to the sea. Stavros had told Alexander that a hotel was planned on a nearby beach, next to an important archaeological site, the Byzantine village called Monemvasia, a jumble of houses on a promontory connected to the mainland, where small houses climbed up to a church at the top of the mountain. But the most startling news for this village of Sekea was the possibility that electricity would be brought to them. Stavros had been the mayor who had been negotiating this new development.

I did not want electricity to come here. I loved our way of life, the dark nights but the skies encrusted with stars, the quiet. I like the darkness best, and that time just before darkness. There are no doubts then, just belief in whatever lies underneath the dark. I prefer not to see the eyes of those who will try to look with jealousy or with evil intentions. Sometimes harm is not at all intended —but it comes anyway. Just a glance—that is all it takes.

I love cooking on a fire or on coals. I do not even mind using the outdoor toilet; I keep mine clean and free of insects. Eventually, the outside world will bring something else: lack of belief in my abilities.

As I sat outside my house that evening, I feared the loss of all that I loved. I wanted every night to be like this: the shadows slowly growing and the setting sun making the small houses glow red. This was the time between light and dark when anything seemed possible. And just when the darkness brought a threat of fear and blindness, the moon and stars would miraculously appear. Now, I faced my own guilt. I had wanted Stavros dead. His plans were changing my way of life. But I did not kill him. I watched the sun slip behind the mountain, lit my oil lamp, and prepared for bed.

When I finally slept that night, I dreamed that Maria was standing in front of my house, pointing at the full moon, a small girl clinging to her leg. I woke up and looked out the window: the moon was still a small sliver in a sky covered by stars.

I woke again when I felt someone slip into my bed. My lover Yiannis, a widower, often visited me at night. He held me now and let me sleep. In the morning he was gone. I didn't want anyone to know that I had such a friend. It would make me seem too "normal" for a woman who healed and knew spells.

In the morning I walked to Chrysoula's house. People were gathering to offer their sympathy. The priest, Father Nectarios, was sitting outside the house, greeting villagers, who stooped to kiss his hand. He made the sign of the cross many times. Our eyes met, but he did not acknowledge me. I walked past him and entered the house.

Alexander had arrived and stood beside his father's body. Chrysoula was sitting next to him, crying softly. The table was stacked with food and drink brought in by women of the village. I kissed Chrysoula and she again whispered to me her request: "Katina, please find out who did this. I will pay you."

She started to wail again and said to me, "I knew we were going to have bad luck. It was because of that foreign girl who came, that Maria, who claimed to be related to us. I knew she would cause some catastrophe."

"This was not her fault," I told her. "Please believe me. Someone else purposely killed your husband." Chrysoula continued sobbing.

I went outside and looked at the people gathered there. There was Yorgos, the village clerk, who had worked closely with Stavros. He was an intelligent man, who had attended the secondary school, the *gymnasio*. He liked to read novels, though they were hard to come by. His son in Athens sometimes sent him books and Yorgos shared them with me. We enjoyed discussing them. I did not believe that he was a killer. His wife Penelope was there, too—a kind woman, but not as intelligent as her husband. I think she resented my friendship with her husband.

There were also Evangelios, builder of houses; Nikos, proprietor of our one taverna; and Kyria Kalliope, an attractive widow who had isolated herself since her husband had died two years ago. When I saw Pericles coming, I almost left, but stopped myself. I was being paid to investigate this crime and must stay. Pericles and I had been sweethearts years ago, but he had, instead, married Marika, daughter of the priest. He had had little choice, due to his parents' wishes, but I thought he had been much too willing to marry her. Marika was a large-bosomed woman whose hair had been a bouquet of beautiful black curls. After his marriage, Pericles had come to my home several times in the night, but I had always turned him away. Still, I knew that Marika was jealous of me and had always suspected that her husband still loved me. She walked by me with her husband, stopping to kiss her father as she passed by, but ignoring me. Her mother, Eftihia, was now standing behind her husband, looking sadly at all those who had come. Pericles glanced at me and winked. I couldn't help but smile. I had missed him at first but had accepted my fate.

I had been considered unmarriageable because my parentage was a mystery. I had been left at the home of our former priest, Father Konstantinos, who, though celibate, with no wife to assist, had raised me, with the help of his housekeeper, the kindly widow Demetra. I had a happy childhood, but, when I came of age, people wanted to keep their sons away from me. They did not know who my family was, or whether I might be related to them.

It was suspected that my mother was a young woman who had disappeared several months before my birth and abandonment. She had been called Haroula, Joy, and had always had a cheerful personality. She was never known to have had a boyfriend. No one knew what had happened to her. Somewhere in this village was my father, or at least I had always believed that. But no man ever looked at me with shame or even fatherly concern.

Now I was 52 years of age and the mystery of my heritage did not matter any more.

That night I delighted in Yiannis's embraces, and forgot, for a time, my assignment. But early in the morning I was there at the church to honour the passing of Stavros Yorgopoulos, the man who wanted to lead our village into modernity.

Father Nectarios chanted the beautiful words I loved. At the end, everyone filed up for the last kiss, leaning over Stavros to kiss him and make the sign of the cross — or perhaps just to touch him and cry. One elderly woman, a stranger, hung behind. She turned and walked away. I went looking for her but she had disappeared.

I wondered whom Stavros would visit tonight. He would walk for forty days, visiting all those he had known. The village would be quiet, without music or dancing, until this time was over. I did not expect him to visit me. I was uneasy that night, however. Though the darkness usually comforted me, I thought I heard whispering and I smelled something, the scent of a kind of soap that I did not use. A breeze made my curtains flutter. I lay there waiting, but Stavros did not materialize. Still, I felt his presence.

I slept but something woke me. A tapping on my door, the rear door of my small house. This was real tapping, I thought, not the whisper of a ghost. I opened the door to a stranger, perhaps the elderly woman I had seen at the funeral.

"Please let me come in," she said quietly. "I am Haroula."

I held up my lamp and looked at her face. I knew that I was staring at my own mother.

"The Virgin Maria told me that I must come to see you," she said. "I arrived to find that Stavros had died. But I am glad that you are here, alive, thriving."

I began boiling water for a small coffee, a *kafethaki*. My mother sat there at my table, looking at me sadly. "I am so sorry to have missed your life, my daughter. But I have always loved you. I regret that I couldn't be here. I was going to confront Stavros, your father, who raped me when I was a young girl. But I was too late."

Stavros was my father. The man who had been threatening my livelihood, my very existence, had also been responsible for my conception. I could not speak for a long time.

"I am sorry." My mother took my hand. "He never

46

knew that he had a daughter. I told only my mother and Father Konstantinos, who adopted you. My mother was Demetra, the woman who raised you."

I cried then. I was happy that Demetra had been my grandmother. She had made my childhood a happy one.

"But why did you leave?"

"Stavros' father knew that he had raped me. He forced me to leave—but I secretly brought you back to my mother. I had no money and had to work as a servant to a family in Sparta. Eventually, I married a local man and we moved to Canada. He would not have married me if he had known that I had a child, that I was not a virgin."

After two hours, my mother left me. I lay in bed but could not sleep that night. The shadow of a man, hanging, kept swinging back and forth on my wall.

In the morning sun, it seemed that everything had been a dream. I walked to the *agora*. Villagers were gathered around two men in suits who were standing in front of a large black car. They were here, they said, to discuss with the mayor the plans for bringing electricity to the village. Panayotis took them to Yorgos in the village office. Soon the men went away, asking that they be informed when a new mayor had been chosen.

That night I heard a whisper coming from my window as I lay in bed. A dark shape was standing there. "Who is that?" I cried out. The shape floated in. "Stavro, leave me alone. I do not want you as a father. Go away!" The shadow floated back through the window. I had hoped my mother would return, but she did not. I told no one, not even Yiannis, about my visitors.

In the morning, to my surprise, Father Nectarios came to my door. I politely made him a *kafethaki* and sat with him on my veranda. He admired my plants, thriving even in the dryness. "You must be wondering why I am here," he said. I did not reply.

"We must work together to keep away the modern world. It is a world of evil and blasphemy. If we get electricity, soon television will come and then people will lose their faith. This will hurt you, too. Not just the church. I would not normally make a bond with you. I always thought you were connected to the devil. But I see that you have done much good for the people of this village. And you are the lesser of two evils." He sipped his coffee, some drops landing on his long beard. I wondered how he could stand wearing the heavy black garment in this heat. His hair was tied back but loose strands fell on his neck. His face was creased with worry.

"Father, I believe in the church. My views are not so different from yours. But I have other beliefs, ones that the church has condemned, for fear of losing its power. I, too, fear the electricity. But we cannot stop it forever. It is destined to come to us. All we can do is to try to persuade people to have faith in the old ways."

"We must do more. Think of something," he said. He got up, knocking over his chair, and stalked off. Then he turned back. "And please stay away from my son-in-law. Stop tempting him."

I did not want to help him, after that final comment. And all I knew were herbs and spells—words used to influence events. Father Nectarios did the same thing, but he would not admit that. So, I burned incense and spoke words of power, though I did not think that these would be enough.

Life resumed as if nothing had happened. My mother did not return. Chrysoula went into seclusion. Alexander returned to Australia. Father Nectarios prayed in his church and spoke on Sundays about the evils of the modern world. Yiannis came almost every night to my bed. People came to me for help against the evil eye. I tried to forget that Stavros was my father.

Sunday morning I woke up to screams. I threw on my housedress and followed the screams to the church. Eftihia was yelling for help from inside the church. I followed the mob inside—and there was Father Nectarios, lying in blood on the altar. I pushed through the bodies and knelt to check his pulse. It appeared that he had been stabbed with a kitchen knife. I could not examine him closely, however, for Eftihia spat on me. "It is you. You caused this. You with your old ways, defying the church yet daring to show your face inside this building. Because of you, no one tried to bring a real doctor here. I know who you are—the bastard of the whore Haroula. That is all you are."

When I felt no pulse, I stood up and walked out of the church. I returned to my bed and cried until I slept. I saw my mother in my dream, crying for me, reaching her arms out. "It was not your fault," I exclaimed. "It was Stavros, that evil man. I'm glad he is dead."

My mother disappeared and I saw eyes, only eyes, glowing red, burning holes in the darkness.

In the morning Panayotis brought me a letter. It was from Canada, from a lawyer's office. Inside was news I could not believe. A letter from my mother, telling me about my conception and birth, about Stavros, all the things she had already told me. There was a note with the letter: "We regret to inform you that your mother died before she could mail this letter. We are sending it to you. It was not found immediately; the burial has already taken place, nine months ago. Her husband died before her, and we did not know that she had a daughter. We are sorry that you were not informed sooner. Please accept our condolences." She had been dead well before she came to visit me.

Had I seen this letter before? Had I dreamed her return to me? Had I cast the evil eye on Stavros? Had I caused the death of the meddling priest?

The night was dark. There were not so many stars as before. The moonlight was pale and weak.

A rustling woke me up that night. I reached for Yiannis, but he had not come tonight. Someone was there, though, standing beside my bed, staring at me. The shadow on the wall showed someone in a black cassock, someone with long hair and a scruffy beard. "Father, why are you here? I cannot help you. Please go away."

"I have to confess to someone, and God will not listen. He knows my sin. I will now burn for eternity."

"I know of your sin, Father. You knew that Stavros was a rapist, yet you kept silent. You did not help my mother or me."

"I know. That is true. But I am speaking of a much

worse sin. It was I who murdered Stavros. I asked him to meet me that night. I begged him to prevent the coming of electricity, but he laughed at me. 'You can't hold back time,' he said. And he called me old man, I, a priest, and the man who had never told about his crimes. Your mother was not the only woman he raped—and I had kept silent. 'I never told of your sins,' I said to him. He replied, 'Sins! Is it a sin to find pleasure in a young woman's body? Your ways are old-fashioned. Leave me alone, old man.'

He laughed again. In my anger, I reached out and grabbed him by the throat. My fury must have given me strength. He tried to fight me off, but he was tired and weak from working all day in the fields. I had not planned to kill him, but I couldn't stop. When I saw that he was dead, I went for help. One man who respects me—I won't name him—helped me hang him from the rope that was still there, hanging down from the branch of the tree where we hang animals when we clean them. I told him that Stavros had tried to kill me and that I had needed to defend myself. He swore in God's name that he would never tell anyone that I had killed Stavros. We placed an overturned chair beneath him. I thought that people would think he had committed suicide. God forgive me."

I was unable to speak for a few minutes. "But who killed you ..." I could not say "father." "Who killed you, Nectario?"

"I did it with my own hand, the worst sin of all. I will burn and burn."

I thought I smelled fire, saw smoke blowing out of his beard.

I sat up to look more closely, but there was only emptiness where he had stood. I sat up the rest of the night, drinking cool water that I had brought in from my well, wondering what I should do. This was something I would not tell. The truth would destroy the villagers' faith.

༄ The days passed, but the villagers were still quiet, looking suspiciously at each other, not daring to trust their former friends. The murders were still a mystery to almost everyone. The summer was hot and dry. I was fanning myself outside my house when I saw flames. The forests in the mountains were burning. Flames were leaping down the mountain, reaching for our village. A spark leapt onto my bare foot, sputtered and went out. Yiannis and I filled buckets with water and fought the flames back. Everyone in the village was doing the same. We did not want to leave. A few people filled bags with their belongings and started along the road on donkeys, in carts, or in old decrepit cars. Most of us were still fighting the fire. Finally, I packed my herbs and potions, my goat and chickens, and filled Yiannis' wagon with all I could. I ran around my house saying the words of power, of protection. Ancient words that most people had forgotten. I buried my icon of the Virgin Mary with my statue of Dionysus in the dirt in front of my door. I prayed that they would keep my house safe.

A lone helicopter flew overhead. Then two planes, spraying. Still, the fires roared. My eyes were stinging. I was coughing. Yiannis handed me a handkerchief. We covered our faces as we rode away. Down the mountain.

To the sea. We had nowhere to go. We stared out at the sea, watching the sunset trying to break through the dense smoke, the blackened sky.

When we were able to return, my house was still standing, but scorched along one side. I dug up the icon and the statue, and set them up inside. The villagers were slowly filing back, some of them finding burnt clothing and furniture in their houses. But we were all safe. We were all still here. The village had not been destroyed. Though the church was damaged by smoke, the priest's Bible and the icon of the Virgin Maria survived.

༄ Yiannis and I are married now. Everyone is happy for us. He is building another room onto my tiny home so that there will be space for his belongings. I could never leave this place.

I have told no one about Nectarios' confession.

༄ It is months later. Everyone in the village has gathered in the *agora*. Voices shout and hands applaud as something zings across the wires, competing with the sun, bringing heat and light. It will dim the stars. Yorgos, the mayor, turns on the first electric light in the village. It illuminates his office, the papers on his desk. He will be able to work at night now. He will be able to read for many more hours each day. Perhaps that is why he agreed to sign the papers. Already men are working to bring one outlet to each house. Eventually, we will cook on electric stoves—though I don't know who can afford to buy one. People are already planning to open tourist shops, to sell hand-knit sweaters, homemade goat cheese, and warm bread.

We do not have a priest yet to bless this event. Father Nectarios would certainly not have done so. His widow, Eftihia, stands beside the church, watching the celebration. She hangs her head and walks away. She has not entered the church since the death of her husband. Perhaps she knows that he was a murderer, that he had committed the unpardonable sin of suicide.

I grow older. Yiannis and I spend all our days and nights together. Some people still come to me for my herbs and spells. I worry that my work and my life are coming to an end. I am cooking over my fire when a woman comes to my door. Behind her is a young child, a girl. "*Yiasou*," she calls. I look closely. My sight is weakening now. "I am Maria. Remember me?"

"Ah, yes, please come in." They enter my dark house and sniff my potions and herbs.

"It smells wonderful in here. Fresh. Natural."

"I am so sorry about your husband."

"How did you know?"

"I knew."

"I heard the bad news about my cousin Stavros. Do you know who killed him?"

"The gods. But he won, anyway."

Maria smiled. "No, he didn't win."

She turned to her daughter. "Meet my daughter Demetra. Demie, this is Kyria Katina. She has much to teach us."

Demetra's smile is angelic. She asks me, in Greek, for a drink of water. "It is hot," she says.

"Yes. It will cool down now. The sun is about to set."

I reach over the table and pull the string attached to my one light bulb. Yellow light makes a circle on the table.

Maria reaches up and pulls the string again, leaving us in dusk. "Do you still have your oil lamp?"

I smile and go to the hearth, pick up the lamp, bring it to the table, and light it.

"Have you met the new priest?" Maria says. "He is my cousin. His name is Dionysus."

I hear Yiannis working outside. He will not disturb us. Three women, with eyes so sharp they can pierce the darkness.

Paved

the day they paved the *agora* I stayed inside my house   I smelled the cement   heard dirt calling out earth trapped underneath   prison bars coming down machines rolled through streets   dirt will not choke us in the heat or in the wind we are told   people will not get muddy in the rain

the mayor left his television show to walk to the edge of the square   a monument will be built to the war dead so many names   my father   my grandfather   my brother   a tribute   I don't need it   they are always with me   the dead call out from the earth that is trapped now underneath cement

the owner of the grocery store is building a new house   up the mountain   with air conditioning   now there are telephones in every home   televisions in some of them   my grandfather had a bagpipe made of a goat's bladder   he would play it in the old dirt square and we would dance   we would sing the old songs   now our children sing American songs and leave our village as soon as they can   they want the new American music the clubs   even the drugs

I heard the machines paving our village our customs our music our laughter   turning them to concrete

but I am still here   people still come to me   the living and the dead visit me   the old ones will never forget sleeping on the roofs of our small houses in the summer heat   catching the breeze   eating almonds from the tree watching the chickens walk along the streets   free as we once were   coming home to eat   children running through the streets up and down the hills   always safe

the day they paved the *agora* people gathered in excitement   children pointed to the men in hard hats and to their big machines   from a dirt courtyard we could hear old folksongs played on a record player   Kyrios Angeletakis came home from milking his goats up the mountain   stopped to stare   carefully carried the warm milk around the vehicles toward his house where his wife and children were waiting   the widow Psihoyiou sang at her window a song about a man drowned at sea a baby was crying down the road   the rooster crowed over and over again for a dawn that would never come

the door to the *taverna* was blocked by the paving men climbed into the back window to sit inside and drink ouzo   old Barba Yiannis needed someone to lift him up and someone else to drag him inside   he limped to the chair and swallowed his first ouzo in one thirsty gulp   I did not see this but Lefteris told me when he came to my bed that night   Lefteris had seen it all   the paving the drinking the laughter   the old men in the *taverna* hiding their fear in glasses of ouzo   the paving so ugly and white and hard   they even paved the entrance to the priest's outhouse   the Pater worries about urine dripped on concrete   smelling   not absorbed into the earth   he tells his wife she must wash the concrete every day   everyone must wipe with strips of newspaper before leaving the outhouse

cats gathered to watch the men working   birds flew overhead seeing their breakfast worms disappear under hardness   children could not wait   wanted to make their marks with hand or foot in the soft surface   they were shooed away by the men in the hats   a lonely dog looked for a cool spot to lie down in the heat

a temporary fence was erected around the cemented areas   Kyria Dimopoulou's lamb broke through and became trapped in gluey substance   was rescued by laughing neighbours who washed the bleating animal as clean as was possible   the frightened lamb went running to find its mother tied behind the Dimopoulos house

the large cyprus tree that gave shade to the *agora* was cut down before the paving   the concrete will burn our bare feet   the old men will sit in the harsh sun playing *tavli* as long as they can before going home for their afternoon naps

the village oven is gone   the *fourno*   people have their own stoves now   make their bread at home   the taste is not the same   my day at the *fourno* was thursday a little girl followed me home one day   asked me for a piece of the newly baked bread   I gave it to her gladly

a dirt path still leads to my house hidden behind a jumble of others   people who come to me will leave their prints in the dirt   their names their memories their

secrets   held by the dirt absorbed into and under our
village   lasting

they will bury me someday in dirt   they will try to
harden my bones   mix them with chemicals   make
everyone think I was a myth   a poem   I am both myth
and poem   they are true things   visions coming from
the spirit inside   the earth   the body   they cannot pave
my body   my softness does not harden into something
white   something that repels moisture   I will be here

they have paved my village and the roads leading to
my village   they have paved many of the streets   but
some they have missed   dirt paths still wind their ways
into our soft hearts

and I am still here

The Secret Temple

ON A GREEK island, just behind this village, along a path through woods and over rocks, is a small chapel—a new one, brightly whitewashed, standing proudly on this ancient ground as if claiming its victory over the past. The Bishop ordered the villagers to build it in this spot—so they did.

Beside the chapel, lying on its side, is an ancient column, its capital curving in the Ionic style. Yorgos points to it in embarrassment. *We found that when we were digging to build the chapel,* he says. *We had to build the chapel here, the Bishop said so. But if we report our find, we will be put in jail.*

I look in awe at the column but I do not touch it or even photograph it. I, too, fear that he will go to jail—or the villagers will be fined, and they have little money.

The Bishop told you to build the church. Shouldn't he go to jail?

Ah, bishops and priests—they never go to jail. Just us.

Near the church, and the column, is an ancient platanos, or plane tree. Yorgos points out that the thick trunk is the width of five men. I take photographs of the tree and the chapel, but not of the column.

We continue our walk along the path. I stumble over the rocks that almost block our route, picking my way slowly. We pass behind a row of gardens, many of them no longer cultivated, and pastures where people keep their sheep and donkeys, though only a few animals bleat and bray as we pass. Until this year Yorgos' garden was almost magical in the size and taste of its fruit and vegetables. Now he is ill and cannot garden; his land is overgrown, wild.

Yorgos picks a fig from one of the many fig trees along the way, opens it, and offers it to me. The sweet fruit drips down my chin. He tells us that these figs will rot on the trees, for they cannot afford to pick them. Prices on the market are too low to make it worthwhile.

We come back into the village near one of the three tavernas and stop for an ouzo. The owner brings us lamb chops, *horiatiki* salad with large chunks of feta cheese on top, gigante beans, and fried potatoes. The village is peaceful; as the sun sets, we hear children laughing and singing as they run through these safe streets.

This is a village that has survived, that clings to its traditions just as it clings to the mountains surrounding it. Families still live here and milk their flocks of sheep in the early morning and early evening. There are signs, though, of change: houses left empty by families who have moved to cities or to other countries; houses collapsing because owners cannot pay to maintain them;

modern buildings on what was once open ground for grazing goats and sheep.

There are still women who know how to avert the evil eye and how to make medicinal potions. That is changing, too. Years ago when I first came here, I was struggling with a cough I had had for months. I had grown very thin and weak. Women came to me in a dark room, dropped oil into water, looked at the result, and spoke mysterious words I did not understand. The next day my cough was gone.

Several years later, I came back. Again, I had a cough. I was confident that the women would cure me. But when I mentioned my cough to the woman who had previously healed me, she looked puzzled—as if she almost remembered something but couldn't quite think what it was. She made no offer to help me, uttered no words of power. But, for a moment, she hesitated.

When we return to the house, Yorgos shows me an old book with information about ancient civilizations that existed on this island. The location in which this village sits is listed as a place that was occupied in those distant times.

He is filled with anxiety about his decision to keep the discovery secret. On the one hand, he and the other villagers who helped build the church were acting on the instructions of a Bishop. On the other hand, Greek law states that all discoveries of ancient artifacts must be reported. He thinks of the probability that old gods were worshipped where the chapel is now, of the importance to Greece, and to architects everywhere, of those signs of classical civilizations.

I am torn, as well: caught between my desire that the ruins be excavated, so that I, and everyone, can see what is hidden underground—and my fear that Yorgos and other villagers will be fined or imprisoned.

I imagine the possibilities:

Scenario 1: The discovery of the column is reported. Underneath the chapel is an ancient temple. Archaeologists have the chapel moved to a different location and excavate the site. Slowly they discover something beautiful and find relics from the ancient past that will explain much more of that civilization than we have known before. These archaeologists will need places to live and places to eat. The taverna owners will make money. The people will rent out rooms in their houses. They will be able to repair broken walls, renovate buildings, build new houses. Then tourists will come. A hotel will be built, along with new restaurants and clubs, all probably owned by people from Athens. Souvenir shops will open. Though the village will be fined, the money coming in from the archaeologists and tourists will make up for the money lost and will benefit the people. Though the peace and safety of this place will be destroyed, something magnificent will arise from beneath the ground, something smooth and cool to the touch, so old that it will make my fingers tingle.

Will they let us touch it, walk into it? Or will ropes surround it, keeping us back, making us admire it from a distance?

Years ago, there was no electricity: we used oil lamps in the house and when we went outside at night we walked slowly, holding hands, hoping not to trip on the cobble-stones. We would spend the evening swinging on one large swing hanging from a tree—taking turns, with everyone singing old folk songs as the swing was pushed back and forth. Before us the smooth surface of the cliff rose up and turned into a dark ghost as night fell. If the village becomes famous—a place for scholars and tour-ists to visit—the silent darkness, the soft creaking of a swing, young voices singing those haunting traditional melodies, will belong to the past.

Scenario 2: The discovery is reported. The villagers are fined but there is no money for excavations for years to come. The village will go on in its peaceful state, as it always has. But times are changing. People will move away. Children will grow up and leave. There is, after all, no high school here, only a small village school for young children. Already there is a scarcity of donkeys. A vege-table truck comes once a week with fresh produce, since fruits and vegetables are no longer grown here. Most of the people with gardens and livestock are old, their chil-dren gone to Germany or Canada or America or Aus-tralia, visiting once a year, if that. These people can no longer spend hours doing physical work. Already the land is becoming neglected. Reporting the find will not change anything.

Scenario 3: The villagers do not alert the authorities. The column remains, perhaps to be discovered someday by a traveller who takes a photograph and sends it to a friend. The friend puts it on his website. Eventually, someone notices the photograph and seeks out the location of this column. The authorities arrive with a team of archaeologists. No one is fined since no one knows any longer who built the chapel, who found the column, who kept its existence silent.

Scenario 4: The column is never reported; the ancient temple is never discovered. An entire city lies underground, sleeping quietly.

For now, the column sits there beside the chapel. I wonder what god was worshipped here. I wonder if Sappho climbed to this village, to this temple, to worship. I long to see that glorious temple hidden underneath the chapel, buried below layers of earth.

I wish I had touched the fluted column. I wish I had taken one secret photograph.

I will tell no one.

One Hundred Eyes

EATING GRASS. I am eating grass. I don't know why. I remember only his whispering to me, that buzzing in my ear. I chew slowly. My jaw circles around the tough blades. They slip down into my stomach. Why am I so heavy? I try to lift my arms. I lift up one—not an arm, it is a leg, I see a hoof, not the lovely nails my sister painted for me yesterday. Yesterday? Was it all a dream? Am I dreaming now? I still hear the whispering, telling me I am beautiful—and luscious.

This grass is delicious and green. I try to stand up but cannot. I am on all fours, I have four legs, I lie down, legs underneath me, I look at my body. I am not wearing clothing. My skin is rough but white. I am so thirsty. I get up slowly—so difficult—move clumsily to the water. This is the same spring where I always sit, bathe, cool my feet. Looking at myself in the water, I see not a young girl with long golden hair, but some sort of animal. I look more closely. It is a cow. I look behind me, but only I am here. I shake my head from side to side, and the cow shakes its head, too. I try to protest, to cry for help. All that comes out is a low *mmmmmmoooo*.

Zeus whispered. I fled. I knew that his wife would be watching. I hoped she would protect me. I am innocent, love to bathe in the fountain, dance under waterfalls, do not want old men to watch or touch me. No one should touch me, for my father is Inachus, King of Argos. He is a river-god, and my mother is a nymph. I am something between god and nymph. I am human.

But Zeus's rough hand caressed my shoulder, reached down. I fled into the woods. I thought I could outrun him—but I forgot his magic, his power. He reached me, held me down on the ground.

Then we heard her, Hera, shouting. *What are you doing, Zeus? Are you after a young virgin again?* Clouds hid us, but they soon evaporated. How I wished I could fly.

Now here I am. Eating grass. Tied to a tree. A creature with one hundred eyes watching me. In the morning he lets me graze further away. I hear voices, familiar ones, my sisters, how I miss them, I should be with them. I was with them yesterday—or a few days ago—I don't know how long ago it was. We were sitting in the shade of a huge plane tree discussing our future plans. I wanted to travel all over the world, to get an education, to move to the city. I did not want to get married yet. My sisters laughed at me. "You'll never get away with it," they said. "You may be Father's favourite but he already has a man picked out for you." Then the sky grew dark, and I could no longer see my sisters. Something, someone, whispered, chased me, snatched me away.

How I miss my sisters. I hear them calling me. *Io. Io.* They run to a man, my father, he is weeping. *My daughter, my daughter, she must be dead. She should have come home last night. What has happened to her?* I move closer to him, to my sisters. The youngest one reaches out to me, pets my back with her soft hand. *Hello, little heifer. You are beautiful.* She looks into my eyes.

Her eyes are like Io's, Father, and look, she seems so sad.

There is rustling in the woods and the bush behind me begins to sway. *Come, heifer.* The large creature with many eyes is coming for me. My father and sisters start to run away, but I call them. *Mmmmmmooo.* They look back. With my hoof, I make marks on the dirt path — straight line and circle: IO.

My youngest sister looks down. *Father,* she cries. *Come see. Come all of you. It is Io.*

They form a circle around me, look down at my name. My father cries even harder. *My lovely daughter. I had a husband all picked out for you. Now you must marry some rough-skinned bull.* They are crying for me, and I am crying inside. They try to protect me from Argus but he is howling as he tramples down the grass coming for me. He throws a halter around my neck and leads me off. I try to resist but he is too strong.

Now he ties me to a tree and watches me with all those eyes. Eyes that never blink. Two sleep at a time; ninety-eight are always wide open. Those eyes stare and stare — until something happens. The eyelids droop. Soft, haunting music. Hypnotic, haunting pipes playing in ways I have never heard before. I look to see where the music is coming from. Only a glimpse, perhaps a dream —a beautiful god playing the pipes. Hermes. I feel my body relax, as I watch Argus. He is trying to stay awake, but Hermes' music is lulling him to sleep. One eye closes, then another, then another; soon all one hundred eyes are closed. With a sudden stroke Hermes throws a stone at Argus. Argus drops to the ground, dead. Hermes raises a hatchet. With one blow he cuts off Argus' head. I see it rolling, rolling, bouncing across grass, against rocks. Hermes gives the head a kick and sends it over the cliff, spattering blood and eyes as it rolls.

A bright light drops down from the sky—a goddess in all her splendour. Draped in a flowing gown, powerful, angry, Hera slams herself to earth and rushes to the dead Argus. She roars in her fury. She plucks Argus' eyes from his body, and weaves them onto the tail of her pet bird, her peacock. Eyes that do not see. Eyes that glitter when the peacock shrieks and spreads its tail.

The music stops. Hermes is shaking me. *Run*, he says, *run*. I run as fast as my heavy hooves can carry me, run for hours, never stopping, even to sleep. I fear that Hera will follow me. Something does. Something is flying around my body, stinging me—here, there, everywhere. If I only had hands. I run and run, from my home in Argos, north then east through countries that are harsher, more barren. I swim across the Bosporus, I don't know how I can do it, I move my hooves in rhythm, somehow I stay afloat. I travel beside a large sea, then up into high mountains, up to the highest one of all. My hooves dig into the earth as I climb, climbing until I can climb no higher.

I worry that I am losing my human self, truly becoming a cow. My mind thinks only of grass. I seek grass, hate the rocky soil and sharp shrubs. My thoughts withdraw into greenness, but my wondering makes me still human. I wish that I could leave my hardships and become nothing, nothing at all. Where are the gods? Where is my father? Surely he will try to find me.

As my hooves clatter up to the top of the mountain I see something before me — an enormous man, a giant, the largest smooth-skinned creature I have ever seen. A loud clacking makes me jump. The flapping of wings on a creature even more enormous than the giant. The eagle swoops down and starts to gnaw at the man's liver, blood pouring everywhere, the godlike being moaning. I mooo in horror, trying to scream. The eagle finally flies away. I move closer to the man, to see if he is dead. He looks at me. His eyes are filled with pain but there is something hopeful in his gaze.

You have come, Io, he says.

How do you know my name? As I speak, I hear only mooing, but he understands me.

I know many things. His voice is mellifluous, deep, filled with pain.

What horrible thing has just happened to you? How are you still alive?

I must sleep now. My liver will regenerate, then the eagle will return, over and over again.

But who are you? What is your name?

I am Prometheus.

He sleeps and so do I, my legs folded under me, despite the constant stinging of my flesh by the tiny powerful insect sent by Hera.

The next day he tells me his story, that he tricked Zeus with two dishes of meat, that he stole fire from Zeus after Zeus kept it away from humans, that he is being punished by Zeus for giving fire to humans. He supports the mortals, the humans whom Zeus tries to tyrannize.

This is what happens, he says, *if you defy the gods.*

I understand. I defied the gods, too. I refused Zeus and dishonoured Hera. Will an eagle eat my liver, too?

You will have a different punishment. But you must not give up. Good will come to you.

How can you bear the suffering? I ask him. *Do you not wish you could die and end it all? I wish that sometimes myself.*

Ah, yes, but I know something of the future. You must live, Io, for one of your descendants will kill the eagle and free me.

Will I produce a line of cows? Will a cow or a bull rescue you?

No, you will soon be returned to your original form. He sighs. *It is dangerous to defy the gods. But it is worth it. Protect your humanity.*

I do not believe him. I think about leaping off the mountain. But perhaps he is telling the truth.

When the eagle returns I flee, unable to witness Prometheus' agony again. I try to imagine stealing fire, being brave enough to defy Zeus, an eagle eating my liver. I run.

My coarse hide is burning and stinging, my eyes are swollen. I can no longer stand, so I sleep in the darkness when it comes. For many days and nights I travel, my tail flapping to try to catch the stinging insect but never reaching it. I go south, then west. I do not know where I am going but something, perhaps the insect, propels me in this direction. I lie on the banks of rippling rivers. I cross a desert where I can find no shade, no grass. Finally, I come to a large body of water. I try to drink from it but the water is salty. I know I cannot make it across, so I travel north to find a place to cross. Finally, I see land, a small strip of land, and make it to the other side of the sea. I keep on. Sometimes I see people, who look at me somewhat curiously but then look away. It seems that people are accustomed to seeing solitary cows walking along the road.

My journey continues. It is cooler now. I feel a breeze, smell something so refreshing. I sleep, a relaxing sleep, without dreams. When I wake up, I follow the scent. A long river is before me. I see trees and grass. The riverbank is damp, as if there has been flooding. Water bringing foliage and vegetation. Is this a dream? I move closer to the water, I drink, I look at my animal self in the water, and I pray.

Zeus, please help me. Hera, have pity on me, turn me back into a woman. I never wanted your husband's attentions. I would never threaten a marriage.

Somewhere far above her, Zeus hears her cries. He goes to Hera. *Never again*, he promises; *she is no threat to you, I will not touch her, I swear.* He caresses his wife. She slaps his face. *You are lying. You will never stop chasing young virgins. I will help her, but not because of you. She refused your touch. She travelled a long, long distance despite the gadfly I sent to torture her. I see divinity in her. She has the strength of a goddess.*

The itching stops. My body starts to tingle. My hooves become fingers and toes. My arms are white and smooth. I stand up carefully, timidly, perhaps I am dreaming after all. I open my mouth but am afraid to talk, in case it comes out as *moooo*. I think about grass, but have no desire to eat any. *Thank you.* I say it out loud. I am so relieved when I hear the soft human voice of a young woman, myself. Io.

I follow the river until I see something in the distance. I walk toward the blur of colours and movements. As I grow closer, I see a group of people coming towards me: smiling people in colourful robes and bright headdresses. They hold out their hands to me. I stand there, frightened at first and shy. A man who seems to be their leader, a priest perhaps, approaches me first. He bows his head. He says something but I do not understand his language. When he speaks in Greek, I smile in relief. "Welcome," he says. "We have been expecting you."

They lead me to the river where women gently wash my face and hands. *What river is this?* I ask the priest.

It is called the Nile.

He takes my hand and guides me to a brightly-coloured chariot. I am lifted up and placed in the chariot.

He sits beside me and the horses draw us along the river. All the others follow behind us, singing in their language something that sounds sacred and mystical. We follow the river for a long time. Then I am helped out of the chariot by kindly people and led to a small boat. We travel a short distance. I see ahead of me something that looks like a mirage—an island of palm trees and purple mountains. We float through the gates until we reach shore and disembark. Another chariot is waiting for us— one painted with pictures of gods and priests. I am led to a glorious temple with columns and walls painted with many bright colours. We walk through this huge stone building, through room after room, many with statues and sculptures, to the centre chamber, the sacred place of the goddess. Several priests are there, waiting for us.

They think I am a goddess, a miracle, and they seat me in front of a statue that resembles me. A goddess with cow's horns. People come to worship me. Isis, they call me. Goddess of fertility. They believe I brought flooding to the land and saved the crops. They feed me with fruit and wines, fresh juices, grains and spices. They bow to me. I am uncomfortable with that. I, who was once a cow, am revered as a goddess.

But I worry that I am sick. Perhaps eating grass has poisoned me. Every morning I vomit into the earth. I am feeling heavier. I fear that I am a heifer once more, look down, but see slim legs. I hold out my arms, test my fingers. I look at my belly. It is larger and rounder, and my breasts are fuller. I confide in a priestess, a woman with kind eyes who has the gift of healing. She touches my belly and asks me questions. Then she smiles and tells me that I am expecting a child.

Zeus did not rape me but he touched me, just his hand to my belly, caressed me, lifted my dress to touch my bare skin. That is all he did. I am still a virgin. But now I am with child, his child. I pat my stomach, soothe the baby inside me. It will be all right, I tell him silently.

The months go by. The Egyptians are so happy that I will be a mother, that I, a virgin, will give birth to a new god. They feed me and care for me. I am fertile—like the Nile River. I will bring prosperity to the country.

My labour is not long, not at all painful. I hold my son so closely. I have never known such love. I sleep with him in my arms every night, rock him, kiss his beautiful face. I do not dare put him down, am afraid to sleep. I fear the wrath of Hera if she knows that I have given birth to Zeus' son. I name him Epaphus, "touch," born from the touch of Zeus.

I do sleep finally, but when I wake up, he is gone. I search frantically, calling his name, asking for help, but no one can find him. I know that Hera has taken him. She is angry at her husband, will not allow me to raise my son. But I will not lose Epaphus. I will travel the entire world if I have to until I find him. I set out across the desert, search for years, travel many miles, through blazing heat and unbearable cold. I pray to the goddess Rhea, Zeus' mother, who protected him from his own father, Cronos. She is my son's grandmother. She is the mother of us all. I beg her to save my baby from harm and to bring him back to me.

I return to that piece of land and cross to the other side of the sea, walking east, then north. In my mind I hear drums, cymbals, singing, feet stamping on the earth. I follow that strange music. Finally, after days of walking, my skin sunburnt, my face moistened by tears, I hear music, music that is outside of my mind. I follow until I see a passageway guarded by two lions. I hesitate. Will they devour me? I look cautiously at each one—then I keep my eyes straight ahead and walk through. The lions do not move, though I hear their heavy breathing.

Men are dancing; women, too, dancing, dancing to the sound of throbbing drums. They are dancing around something, somebody. I draw close. They do not stop, so I peer through the gap between two dancers. I see a little boy, dressed in ceremonial clothing. He is sitting cross-legged on the ground. His eyes look both frightened and proud.

When he sees me, he calls out. *Who are you?* The dancers move aside, are stilled by my presence.

I am Io, I call out. *Io.*

The dancers look at me and then at the boy.

Mother? he asks. *I was told you would come.*

He is so handsome. Tears come to my eyes. I approach slowly. *Do not fear, my son*, I tell him. *You are the son of Zeus.* The dancers and their goddess have hidden him from me but now they know that the time has come for me to take him home.

Epaphus, I say, and hold out my hand. He takes it and we start the long journey home. Home—home is now Egypt, not Greece. I know that that is where our futures lie.

Finally, I find love and a man who wants to marry me.

I marry Telegonus, King of Egypt, who will treat Epaphus as his own. My son will achieve greatness, for his father is the most powerful of the gods, and his stepfather is the king of Egypt. Epaphus will become King someday, will be the founder of a great city.

Sometimes I still dream of grass, its fresh smell, its soft texture, its bitter taste. Here, where I live now, there are only sand and some stubbly plants that rip your fingers if you touch them. Sometimes I feel a growling sound deep within my stomach. *Mmmmooooo.*

I live in the desert, but near the Nile River, the fertile crescent. Though the waters of this river are refreshing, they are not the cool springs of Greece. Someday my descendants will return to Greece, the place I still long for but will never see again. There are some who worship me, but I am not a goddess. I am Io. I reach out my hand, so grateful that I have fingers. Every morning I paint my toenails, delighting in feet, in hands, in my soft skin.

Sometimes at night I hear a mournful cry, the ugly screaming of the peacock, whose tail is covered with eyes that no longer see. But when he struts by me in the morning, I see that he is beautiful, his tail spread out in splendid glory—beautiful but impotent. All he can do is shriek and strut.

Now I am sitting quietly with my granddaughter, telling her the story of my life, teaching her what it means to be human.

"What was it like to be a cow?" she asks.

I crouch on all fours. *Come, let's be cows together.* We pretend that we are eating grass.

Moo, I say.

Moo, she repeats.

Let's do it again, Yiayia.

We stoop and munch at air.

Mmmm, delicious, I say.

Mmmooooo, she answers.

I tell her about Greece, my homeland.

Are there cows there? she asks me.

Oh, yes, I answer.

Will you take me there someday?

I do not tell her that I will never go back there. I know that she will go there with her sisters. *You will live there someday* is all I tell her. *You will be fine. Pray to Aphrodite, and do not allow yourself to be tied up. Beware of arrogant gods.*

Is there grass there? she asks me, mooing happily.

Yes. It is very green and very tasty.

Are there monsters?

When I lived there, there was a giant creature with one hundred eyes and every eye could see.

Is he still there?

No, he is gone, conquered by music. His eyes cannot see us now.

What about the giant you saw on the mountain?

He will be saved by someone in our own family.

Good! She smiles.

We sing together, dance on all fours, nibble at invisible grass.

The Cave of Lust*

DARKNESS. DEEP INSIDE the rock. Tunnel that never ends. I do not dare go any further. I hide in the corner, hoping he will not find me. I hear breathing at the cave entrance, step back a little further, touch something soft, almost scream but cover my mouth with my hand. The soft object moves and gasps. "Shhh," I say.

After a few minutes, the creature at the cave entrance moves away, and I turn toward the soft thing behind me. "What is it? Who are you?" I ask.

"Just me, an old person here, just nothing, a thing, a piece of scrap, a used rag, hardly even a woman anymore, but still a woman, still with all parts of me intact and somewhat functioning. I am here to save you. When he comes for you, I will go to him, satisfy his desires, keep him from devouring you."

"Why would you do that?"

"I was once you. Someday you will be me."

I don't know what she means but I am quiet.

---

* This story was inspired by an episode in Edmund Spenser's *Faerie Queene*, Book 4, Canto 7.

"Sleep now," she says. "He won't come back for a while."

So I do. I sleep but dream of a caged beast, playing the bars as if playing a xylophone. He has forgotten to ask for his freedom. He just plays music.

The old woman shakes me. "Wake up, here eat something while you can."

I take what she hands me, put it in my mouth. It is as hard as a rock. I take it out of my mouth with a gasp.

"Hold it in your mouth for a few minutes. It will soften. It's just bread. I'm sorry I don't have anything else. But there is water. He always brings fresh water."

Once the bread is softened, it is not bad. I chew it and swallow it. I'll need my strength. Somehow I'm going to get out of here.

"Tell me who you are," I ask her.

"Nobody, really. He took me from my parents, brought me here when I was young. I've belonged to him ever since."

"How terrible! Did you never try to escape?"

"At first. But, now, this is my life. I can help others, the young, the virgins. It is not your time yet. I will let him take me, and you can run away."

A roaring fills the cave. Something dark is blocking the entrance. He is huge and terrifying, a dark shadow, a beast, he is death. "Is he death?" I ask the woman.

"The death of innocence, he is. But not death to life. He lets you keep on living. That is worse than death."

He is moving towards us. I shrink back into the darkness. The old woman pushes me behind her and whispers, "Hide." I go as far back as I can. I feel the earth behind me and find a blanket, crouch underneath it.

"Where is she?" he asks. "I want her. It's her turn!"

"Not yet," the old woman tells him. "She is too weak and tired. Give her a chance to get her energy back. You don't want a limp rag. There's no pleasure in that. Take me —I'm feeling vigorous today." She moves toward him. He reaches for her and pulls her toward him.

"Shh, not here," she says to him. "Let's go outside, under the apple tree. Let her get her rest. And the fresh air invigorates me."

He gurgles in pleasure, and they walk outside.

I crawl out of the blanket and creep to the cave entrance. I peer outside. The light blinds me. Where are they? I see grass, trees, sun reflecting off a pond. I scutter out, stand up, and run.

I pass an apple tree and hear grunting behind it. I cannot resist. I stand behind the thick trunk and look around it. The two of them, monster and crone, are entangled in each other, bouncing up and down, rolling in the grass, shrieking in laughter. She tears off his shirt, revealing rough skin; he lifts up her shirt—her breasts hang wrinkled down to her belly. He laughs as he caresses her. Then she looks right at me, over his head, and winks. She is singing a song:

> Little girl lost, and little girl found,
> Old girl cavorting on the ground,
> Young and old, virgin and crone,
> Statue or pleasure, together, alone.

I turn away and run toward the pond. I am so thirsty. I lean over and cup my hands in the water, bringing up cool satisfaction to my mouth, washing my face. I look at my reflection. Long, blonde hair. Pale skin. Bright blue eyes. So pure. A ghost.

I turn away from the pond, and walk back, tiptoe past the apple tree, crawl back into the cave. I cover myself with the blanket and sleep, dreaming of golden apples and soft grass. I feel myself growing old.

The Changeling's Brother*

THE DOOR, THE wooden door to the small house. The door I once painted green, like the grass. The paint is peeling now, faded, like the meadow in autumn. Should I knock? Will my mother remember me? Twenty years ago I left home to be a soldier. Now I am back. She must have heard my footsteps. The door opens. A small woman. I barely recognize her. Her hair is grey and tied up in a tight knot. She used to wear it hanging down— black hair, as black as night. Her eyes are surrounded by wrinkles, her mouth puckered in a frown. She looks at me, curiously, almost hopefully. I sense that she doesn't dare to hope. I hold out my arms. "Mother."

She shrieks and falls onto her knees, touches my legs, stands up slowly, touches my chest, then my hair, caresses

---

* This story was inspired by an English folktale told by Jane Probert in 1908 and collected by Ella Mary Leather in *The Folklore of Herefordshire* in 1912. Titled "The Fairy Changeling" it was republished in *The Penguin Book of English Folktales*, ed. Neil Philip, 1991, pp. 311-312.

my face, almost as if she is blind and wants to know every detail of my features. Then she looks into my eyes.

"Is it you, Johnnie? Is it really you?"

"Yes, Mother. It is. I'm home."

"I thought you were dead." The tears run down her cheeks. "Come in. You are home."

She embraces me then, holds me tightly to her chest, her arms wrapped around my back. Finally, she lets go and leads me into the cottage. The place has not changed at all. Wooden table with four chairs around it. Fireplace with a pot hanging over the hearth. Two comfortable chairs beside the fireplace, and another chair in the corner by the door. The fire is unlit right now. It is afternoon. Still warm enough. In fact, the room is stifling. A musty smell makes my nose sting.

I hear a whimper, then a fretful cry, like that of a baby. My brother was an infant when I left. Perhaps he is married and has his own child now.

"Who is that?" I ask.

"Surely you remember your brother Willy."

"Willy? He must be twenty years old now."

I notice a cradle in the corner and walk over to it. I lean over to look inside. There is a baby there—not the cooing, giggling, chubby brother I remember but some creature with a withered, old face and wrinkled body. Pale, thin, whining.

"What is wrong with him, Mother?"

"Nothing. He's just fine. He's just a bit sickly, that's all."

I look at him again. He stares at me, his dark eyes

gleaming with malicious craftiness. For a moment, I see a grin, an evil grin, a knowing, adult look. I feel chills throughout my body.

"This is a changeling, mother. We must get rid of him."

"Do not say that about your brother." She runs to the cradle and rocks it back and forth, patting Willy soothingly. "Don't worry, dear. Your brother hasn't seen you in so long. He doesn't understand."

"Mother, why doesn't he sit up and feed himself? He should be talking and walking. He should be outside, cutting branches for your fireplace, or working to bring in money. It's been twenty years since Father died and I left home. He should have gone to be a soldier, gotten married, had his own child."

"He's just a weak one, Johnnie. He's always been like this."

"He was fine when I left. Healthy and strong."

"Here, dear. Sit down and have something to eat. I'll give Willy some porridge."

Mother serves me potatoes and beets from the garden. "I'm sorry, dear, I wasn't expecting you. I don't have any meat. I would have cooked something special. But—there's tomorrow."

"It's okay, Mother. This is delicious." Indeed, I am very hungry and eat everything on my plate.

Willy doesn't stop whining and complaining all through the meal. He wants more and more porridge. Nothing will fill him. Still, he is thin and pale.

"Mother, has the doctor seen him?"

"He used to come by, but he just gave up. Granny Eldridge down the hill comes sometimes, but she's afraid of him. I don't know why."

"Well, I'm afraid, too. This is not normal. Something is wrong."

"I don't believe he is a fairy changeling," she cries. "I know Granny Eldridge does. She wants me to cast him out, so the real Willy can come back. As if I'd throw my own child out into the woods."

After supper, I climb the ladder to the loft where I've always slept. I had wondered, when I was gone so long, if she had turned it over to Willy or done something else with it. But my mother has not changed a thing. I remember the blue bedspread, the white curtains made of coarse material, the brown walls. The wooden shelf holds toys from my childhood—a wooden soldier, a toy train, some blocks, books of fairytales. There is no sign of the young man I had become—but as I grew up I paid no attention to the room. I never collected things or tried to decorate my bedroom but spent most of my days outside. I'd like to add something colourful now—paintings with crimson fall leaves or violet curtains—though I don't plan to stay here long. I hope to find a wife and have my own baby. Not one like Willy—a twenty-year-old infant! I'll be sure to protect my own child and not let any fairies in.

After thirty minutes, there is a timid knock on my door. Mother, bringing me a cup of hot milk. "Here, sweetheart," she coos. "This will help you sleep."

She hands it to me and looks around the room. "I kept everything just the way you like it."

"Well, I'm a grown man now, Mother, so I'll be making some changes while I'm here."

"While you're here? You won't leave us again, will you?"

"I am an adult. I'd like to find a wife."

"I don't know of anyone good enough for you," she says, with alarm in her voice. "The good ones are all married by now."

"Well, maybe there is a nice widow somewhere. Or I could marry someone younger."

"Good night, Johnnie," she says. She reaches up and kisses my cheek. There are tears in her eyes. "I've missed you so much. I'm glad you are home."

In the night, a few times, I hear wailing. Willy is definitely sick — or not human at all.

The next day I walk to the brewery where I once worked to see if there is a job for me. My father was a foreman here for most of his adult life. The owner, Mr. Bell, rushes out to shake my hand. I am pleased that he is still here. He is somewhat stooped with age but still strong and handsome. "It's so good to see you, Johnnie. Welcome home!" He offers me a job right away. "We need someone like you," he tells me, patting my back. I am pleased and tell him I will start the next morning.

He shakes my hand again. "I'm glad you are home. It must have been terrible, fighting in those wars. I bet you had some terrible experiences."

I don't answer him. He can see that I don't want to talk about this and pats my arm before changing the subject.

"Johnnie, how is that brother of yours? Were you shocked to see him? I always thought he would be working here, too."

"Yes, I am terribly worried. I don't know what to do. Mother won't even admit he's sick."

"Do you think he's a changeling?"

"It's very possible."

"Here's a way to find out for sure. You remember Granny Eldridge? She knows how to detect changelings. Your mother won't listen to her—but I suggest you visit her."

It seems silly to be frightened of an old woman. But as I approach her small house in the isolated countryside just outside the village, my hands are trembling. I remember her as a monstrous-looking person with a big nose—but instead I find a small wrinkled woman, who smiles at me in recognition.

"Johnnie. How wonderful that you came home. I told your mother that you would return someday."

She invites me into her cosy house and serves me hot tea and warm biscuits. We eat silently, until she asks, "You must be here about your brother." I nod.

"Your mother's obsession with him is not healthy. I do believe he is a changeling. Would you like to find out?"

Changelings. Fairy children substituted for healthy human ones. As a child, I was told many stories about fairies. I thought they were just fantasy tales—until one night when I lost my way walking home through the woods. It got dark so suddenly. I was sixteen then, wondering what my future would be, and ready for adventure. Music—faint—little bells tinkling. Lights twinkling in the clearing. Beautiful people, tall and slim, dancing in a circle. Elegantly dressed, the men in old-fashioned green suits and the women in long green gowns. A beautiful woman, her long golden hair falling down her back, reached out her hand to me. The circle opened to admit me. I was ready.

Then something pulled me back. My father. He dragged me home, scolding me the whole time. He told me that had I joined the dance, I would never have come home, would never have been free. Trapped in the dance, circling the ground forever. "Don't tell your mother," he said. I never knew why he said that.

The fairy woman haunted my dreams every night after that. I longed to go back to find her. I spent many sleepless nights planning my escape out my bedroom window, my journey through the woods, my meeting with the woman, who would hold out her arms and embrace me. In the morning, my world seemed drab and dull.

A few months after my encounter with the fairies my father died in his sleep. Perhaps the fairies took him, but they left no substitute father. Was it my fault for almost entering the dance? Was it my fault for not dancing with the fairies? I used to wish that my father was still alive, living a carefree life in Fairyland, that the body we buried had been a changeling.

I left home a month later, though my mother cried and hung onto me desperately and my baby brother looked at me sadly with his deep brown eyes. I don't know when the fairies came to take my baby brother, leaving this sick creature in his place. Perhaps soon after I left—my punishment for abandoning my family when they needed my help. My plan was to make money to send back to them. Instead, I walked through fields of blood, day after day, night after night. Often I slept surrounded by corpses. If only I had joined the fairy dance. On cold nights, in muddy fields, I thought about the life I could have had in fairyland, dancing with that beautiful woman with her golden smile. I remembered the warmth in her glowing eyes—imagined, I realize now, for her eyes were cold, a cold that was somehow inviting. I longed for her.

⁊ Back at work in the hopyards now. This feels safe and familiar—my body enjoys the physical exertion of productive work—so different from the agony of those years hiding and fighting, when I tortured and was tortured. Every evening now, I return home to a hot meal cooked by my mother—fresh vegetables from her garden, potatoes dripping with butter, and often chicken or sometimes lamb. I always offer to help her with cleaning up but she won't let me do anything. She waits on me as if she is my servant. But she frequently leaves my side to tend to Willy—or the creature that she thinks is Willy.

All night, every night, Willy cries and whimpers. I sleep with my pillow over my head but I can still hear him.

⁊ This Sunday my mother wants to go to church to hear a well-known preacher's sermon. I offer to babysit.

This will give me a chance to try the trick for detecting changelings. I have planned ahead so that I have all the supplies I need.

After she goes, I mix together the barley, yeast, and hops, as if I am making beer—but first I gently crack an egg, leaving the shell almost intact, and pour out the egg. I place some of the mixture in the eggshell, then hold it over the fire as I stir.

A strange sound comes from Willy. I look at him. He is sitting up in the cradle and laughing. "What a sight," he says, in a strange adult voice. "I am so old but I never saw anyone brewing beer in an eggshell."

"Ah, so you can talk, can you?" I say. "Tell me who you are."

"Give me a bit of whiskey, and I will."

I pour whiskey in a small glass and hand it to him. He swallows it in one gulp. "Ah, I've been longing for that. Give me a smoke of your father's pipe."

The pipe is still on the corner table near my father's chair. I find some tobacco in the box next to it, fill the pipe, and light it. Willy, or whoever he is, puffs on it contentedly for a while.

"Who are you?" I ask him. "You are not my brother, are you?"

He cackles. "I'm no brother of yours."

"Well, then, go back to where you came from."

I grab the walking stick that is sitting by the door and swing it at him. He jumps out of the cradle, runs around and around the room, then heads for the door. In my rage, I come close to striking him on the head—but he opens the door and dashes outside, racing like lightning down the lane. I chase him with the stick held high, running as fast as I can. I want to make sure that he never returns.

When my mother comes home, she smiles and says, "How was Willy? Was he a good boy?" She walks over to the cradle. She screams when she sees no baby there.

"Where is he, Johnnie? What have you done with him?" She frantically runs around the room, peering into every corner. "Where is my son?"

"He was a changeling, after all—just as I told you. I tricked him. He sat up, talked to me, and drank whiskey. Here, see the empty glass? When I challenged him, he jumped out of the cradle and ran out the door. I saw him disappear into the woods—he moved so quickly, I thought he was flying."

"You stupid fool," she says, sobbing into her hands. I sit beside her, my arm around her shoulder. "It's all right now, mother. I'll help you with the chores—and I've got a good job in the brewery. It will be so much easier for you now."

She shakes off my arm and walks over to the cradle, crying, wailing, "Oh, Willy, oh my darling Willy."

The next morning before going to work, I begin throwing out all the childish objects in my room. I will repaint the room—I think about colours. My mother does not get up, so I make porridge for both of us. Before I leave, I go over to her bed. "There's porridge for you, mother. I'll see you after work." She opens her eyes but says nothing.

She is still in bed when I come home. I throw out the porridge and set out some bread and honey. "Come now, mother. You should eat something." She slowly rises from her bed and hobbles to the table. Her face is grey, her hair falling in tangles over her face. I see that she is old, older than I had realized. She sits down but does not eat.

"Well, mother, it's just you and me. Don't worry. I'll take care of you."

I spread honey on a slice of bread and hand it to her. She reaches for it and takes a bite.

"I miss him," she says.

"Of course you do. But think how happy the real Willy is with the fairies. He'll be dancing all day, eating sweet fruit and drinking cool wine. He is waited on by servants who give him everything he wants. You couldn't have done that for him. But I'm here now. We'll be fine."

She nods and takes another bite of bread. I spread some honey on another slice and put it to my mouth. Honey drips onto my fingers, and I lick them. It tastes heavenly—rich, thick, and sweet. This is how it is meant to be.

A knock on the door startles us. I get up from the table, walk to the door, and open it. A fine-looking young man is standing there, dressed in green pants and a white silk shirt.

My mother shrieks. "Is it you, Willy? Is it you?"

"Hello, Mother," he says.

My mother embraces him, weeping, touches his silk

shirt, pats his face. He moves back slightly, then looks at me. "Are you my brother?" he asks.

"Yes, I am."

"Well, we must make the best of this. I've been sent home now. Is there something to eat?"

Mother leads him to the table. They sit down. She takes bread from my plate and spreads it with honey.

Quietly, I leave the house and walk slowly, deliberately, toward the forest.

The Minotaur

FROM EACH HOUSE, I take something. Something small. This time I pluck a bright red rose from the garden. I'll put it in the small vase that I dropped into my purse at the last house I visited. I'll set the vase on the table beside my bed. Later, I'll dry the rose and press it. It was risky to take the vase—mostly I take things whose absence will not be noticed—for example, a cloth napkin from the dining room table or a single sock from a dresser drawer.

I am wearing my one good outfit, an expensive grey business suit I used to wear when I worked at the bank. I am walking through a beautiful home in the Mountview area. But I have to pretend that it is not suitable for me.

"This is over-priced," I say to the real estate agent. "And it doesn't have a laundry room on the main floor."

"Well," she answers, smiling her fake smile, "it does have four bedrooms, two baths, and an extra apartment in the basement. The cedar deck is beautiful, and the grounds are spectacular." She points out the kitchen window, then sweeps her arm to include the room around us. "Do you like this state-of-the-art kitchen?"

"I don't like islands in the middle. I prefer open space."

"Could I show you something else? There's a house just a few blocks from here that does have a laundry room on the main floor."

"Oh, that'd be great. Right now I have to get back to work, but, if you give me your card, I'll phone you later."

"Certainly." She hands me her card but is already looking toward the door. A family of four is entering. She rushes to them, with obnoxious enthusiasm.

I love this house. If only I could afford it—or any house. I've been unemployed for six months and have had to move into a small rented room in a noisy part of the city. My room is over a Chinese restaurant, with food smells (delicious but all-pervasive) wafting up all day. Next door is a hip-hop dance club, with throbbing music all night. I am exhausted from lack of sleep. But I am so bored that I have decided to indulge in my fantasies of being rich, of living in a mansion. I never stick with the same agent twice, in case they realize that I'm not going to buy anything.

I can't afford dry-cleaning so I brush the suit off when I get home and sponge it lightly with a damp cloth. I hang it up on the hook beside the hotplate and put on my old jeans and plain black T-shirt. I get out the real estate paper again and start circling the most expensive houses listed. There is an open house tomorrow in the exclusive Riverview area. I put a large red X beside the listing.

I walk up a long driveway that circles the pillared porch and enormous front doors, splitting off and running in both directions around the house. The porch continues along both sides of the house. I walk to the right, then to the left, to check—yes, this appears to be a real wrap-around porch, something I've always wanted. This is my dream house—it has a tower, a wonderful one, tall and round, with lattice windows on each level. I have always imagined myself writing poetry and reading mysteries while sitting in a circular room that is at the top level of a tower, with a view of forests and perhaps the sea. I feel a familiar ache of longing. I can't wait to get inside.

I'm the first one here. Good. I can explore without interference. This agent is as smiley and white-toothed as the last. She reminds me of a fox stalking its prey. "Hello," she gushes. "May I show you around?"

"Of course. What a gorgeous place!" I am standing in a large, high-ceilinged, marble-floored foyer with a glass chandelier hanging from the ceiling. Rising from the foyer is a beautiful cherry wood staircase that winds around to the second and third floors, with graceful banisters circling the room.

"There are six bedrooms," she says, "and four baths. But let's start with the main floor. You won't be disappointed."

I'm not. The stately dining room with its banquet-sized table. The large, sparklingly clean kitchen. The comfortable family room with its plush beige sofa and chairs and pale green carpet. The sun room, with large windows looking out onto gardens and trees. The library with its elegant fireplace, built-in bookcases, and beautiful oak panelling. Upstairs each bedroom is spacious, with wood floors, windows to the ceiling, and, another of my favourites, window seats. The master bedroom is enormous and the en suite bathroom larger than the room I live in.

Then the tower. If I could live just here, that is all I would ask of life. The ground level could be my living room, the middle level my bedroom, and the top level, with its view of the grounds, my office or study, where I would sit to read and write. I must take something from this tower. I look out the window and point. "What is that hill I see over there?" I say. While she is looking, I take a small skull from the mahogany desk and slip it into my purse. I remember that this is called a *memento mori*.

"Let's look at the gardens now," she says, smiling. This third level of the tower connects to the third floor of the house—a large room with leather sofas, an entertainment centre (with the largest television screen I've ever seen), and soft, bright-patterned cushions spread around the floor. There is another stairway that goes straight down to the kitchen. I would love to have a "back stairs" again. I grew up in a Victorian-era house that had a back stairway leading from the basement to the attic. I remember sliding down those stairs on old mattresses and cushions that we stole from the living room sofa. If only I could go back to those happy days.

The garden is filled with flowers and plants I've never

seen before. The path winds around and around. "This is a maze," the agent tells me. "You have to follow it to the centre, then find your way back. But there are confusing pathways along the way." She leads me through dirt trails surrounded by foliage. I feel that we are going in circles. Finally, we reach a cleared area with a graceful wooden gazebo. We go inside, and I sit down on the swinging sofa, while she sits on one of the benches. I swing back and forth.

"What do you think?" she asks me.

I pause. "I'm quite overwhelmed. I love it. But it might be a bit too large for my needs. I do have a family—husband, teen-aged sons (I lie)—but this is probably too much. Of course, we'd love it. But the price …"

"… is fair," she adds. "You can't find a house like this at such a good price. What is your profession and your husband's?"

"I'm in banking," I say. "And he is a corporate vice-president. Let me speak to my husband. In the meantime, is there something smaller on your list?"

"Yes, indeed. Let's go back inside, and I'll show you some pictures." She leads me back through the maze. I stop to examine a mysterious plant with large green leaves. When I look up, the agent is gone. For a moment, I panic. Will I ever find my way out? I move slowly along the path, but there are other branching paths that I hadn't noticed before. I can't remember which way we came.

The agent re-appears. "I'm so sorry. I didn't mean to lose you. It takes some getting used to. I got lost a few times myself."

"Why did the owner create this maze?" I ask her.

"Mazes and labyrinths date from ancient times. In Greek mythology, King Minos of Crete built a labyrinth to enclose the minotaur, a horrible monster who was half-man and half-bull. Theseus went into the labyrinth to kill the minotaur. Ariadne, the king's daughter, loved Theseus and gave him a ball of thread to carry so he could find his way back out—or he would have been lost forever. He killed the monster and followed the thread. Ariadne saved him but he eventually left her. The god Dionysus found her and married her. That's only part of the story—sorry for the lecture, but I find this maze fascinating."

"You know a lot about mythology."

"I did some research—though I did take a course in mythology when I was at university. The owner of this house is a retired classics professor and scholar. So, to answer your question, he probably created the maze because of an interest in ancient myth and history. He is also a very spiritual man. Mazes and labyrinths were also considered paths to spiritual renewal and rebirth."

"That's interesting," I say.

"Here, let me show you something—if I can find it."

She looks around for a few minutes, walks back the way we came, then takes the path to the right. We wind around once again. I'm beginning to feel frightened and claustrophobic—the tall plants here have shut out the sun. Then, suddenly, we come out into a clearing. "See," she says, pointing.

She is beautiful—a delicate statue carved in marble.

She is holding a marble ball of red thread—the thread flows down but then ends at the bottom of her feet. There are a few marble tears on her cheeks. I go over and touch her—cool—but she almost looks alive.

"Now, I'll show you something else."

I do not want to leave Ariadne, but I follow the agent down another path. I'll have to come back here.

I stay as close as I can to the agent, so I will not get lost. We come to another clearing. A monster, man's body, bull's head. For a moment, I feel that I can't breathe. His horns curl upward and his sneer reveals sharp teeth. He is leaping toward me. I step back.

"Yes, he is scary, isn't he?" the agent says. "Now, look to your right." She points. "See those bushes?" I walk over. Behind the bush is another statue, a beautiful man, poised to attack the minotaur. "Is it Theseus?"

"You got it."

"Wow. Is Dionysus here somewhere?"

"Yes, somewhere. I haven't been able to find him yet. Oh, my. I've forgotten my duties here. There could be other people coming to the house. We should go back."

"Of course. You lead the way—and don't go too fast!"

She laughed. "I won't lose you."

We head back again but my thoughts are with the broken-hearted Ariadne.

The agent gives me some listings of smaller houses and her card. I hadn't caught her name at first. It is Clio Antonakis. I want to speak to her again, but she is busy with another client. I look at the listings for the other houses but cannot pay attention. I long to go back to that maze. Perhaps there is another way in.

I call out to her. "Ms. Antonakis. I'm leaving. But is it okay if I walk around the house just to see the building?"

"Of course." She waves goodbye.

I go out the front door and walk to the right. I follow the driveway around, looking up at the tower and its top floor. The driveway makes a full circle. Behind it are thick cedar trees that are probably hiding the maze. I peer through them but they are tightly packed together and I can't get through. The only way in is through the back door of the house. I'll have to come back another day. Ms. Antonakis will be delirious, thinking I might buy this mansion.

I didn't lie—not completely. I *was* working in a bank, until I was fired for fraudulent withdrawals from the accounts of a rich elderly man and deposits of his money into another man's account. I claimed it was a mistake, a computer error, and they could never prove otherwise. But it was no mistake. I was talked into it by Thomas, my married lover, who had lost money in the stock market. Stupidly, I did it for him. Once I no longer had access to other people's bank accounts, he dumped me.

I have no children. I did lie about that. My one marriage ended in divorce after six months. Now I am struggling to get by, and my unemployment insurance is about to run out. I lie in bed looking at the *memento mori* that I have placed on the table beside the rose. I reach out and rub the small skull. "Remember your end," I whisper.

The next morning, I phone Ms. Antonakis again.

"Please call me Clio." She would be delighted to show me the house again. The same house twice! I'll have to find something else to wear. I head for a consignment store down the street from my room; I sold most of my nice clothes here after I was fired. I find a smart-looking beige pantsuit and a silky sky-blue blouse. Expensive-looking but cheap, though I'll have to eat toast for dinner tonight.

My mother always wore pantsuits with flowered blouses. She wore long dangly necklaces and matching earrings. She liked bracelets, too, delicate ones with silver beads and trinkets. She kept her fingernails long and pointed and painted a bright red. Her skin was flawlessly white and smooth. In the mirror, in my chic pantsuit, I look like her. For a minute, I think that is she, staring back at me. That is good, I think. I'll definitely pass as a rich lady. My mother was classy—not exactly rich but well enough off. She died just last year, after years in a nursing home that took all the money she had left. I'm glad she didn't know what a failure I am.

Clio greets me at the door. "Did you walk?" she asks. I cannot tell her that I do not own a car, that I'd had to come by bus. "I left my car a few blocks down so I could check out the neighbourhood," I say. I am pleased at my cleverness.

"How old are your sons? There are excellent schools in this area."

"I know. That's one reason I'd like to live here. Do you mind if I wander through slowly?"

"Take your time. I'll be in the kitchen. The maid left some coffee for us."

"Does the owner still live here?"

"Yes, but he's travelling right now. He wanted me to take care of the sale."

I want to ask his name but don't. I start to wander, covering all the floors, then enter the tower, climb to the third floor, go through the entertainment room, down the back stairs, and out the back door. But what will she say if I am gone too long? I'll have to fake it. I retrace my steps and come back to the front hallway. I call out. "Clio, I'm sorry, I just had a phone call. One of my clients needs me right away. I'll be in touch tomorrow."

"Okay, I'll wait to hear from you," she calls out.

I open and shut the front door, then climb up the tower again, go through the third-floor room, back down the stairs, and out the door to the gardens. I slip into the maze unnoticed.

Now that I am here, I am nervous. What if I get hopelessly lost? But I must find Ariadne again. I walk along the path and right away find the gazebo. I sit for a few minutes, trying to remember where we turned yesterday. I can see a glimpse of the sky—dark clouds are starting to block the sunlight. Rain and possibly thunderstorms are predicted for today—but the thick bushes should protect me.

I loved running through the rain with Thomas. He took me with him to Florida once. When the weather turned stormy, we were caught on a beach with rising winds and high waves. We ran, panting and laughing, back to our hotel, threw off our wet clothes, and jumped into the large king-size bed. Then his phone rang—his wife. He took the phone into the bathroom. I could hear his voice cajoling, arguing, soothing. When he came out, he said he'd have to go back home right away. Some kind of family emergency. We had to take separate airplanes, in case someone he knew saw us together. I thought that he feared his wife. I imagined her to be an ugly monster —a female minotaur. I saw her once, with him, at a party. She was beautiful—thin and blonde and stylish. I wondered why he would spend time with me. Now I know.

I leave the gazebo and walk back the way I came, then turn left—or should I be going right? I continue to the left, walk and walk, right into a dead-end. This is frustrating! I'm beginning to perspire. So I turn back, back to the main path, I think. Success! Ariadne is waiting for me, patient but weeping, holding the broken thread. I touch the thread. It is marble, too. Red, like blood. How could Theseus have deserted her after she saved his life? I think about him fighting the minotaur, can almost see the monster running at him, its bull-head butting him in the stomach, but Theseus fighting valiantly and conquering him, killing him with his sword. Without the thread, he would never have found his way out of the labyrinth.

I rub the cold, hard thread, following it down to the ground. "I'm sorry for you," I say to Ariadne. "I hope you were happy with Dionysus. But wasn't he the wild god of wine and revelry? Did he leave you at home while he was out drinking and dancing? I hope he loved you." I am crying as I stroke her hand.

I run my hand down the marble thread. It is not

broken after all. There is a real thread, made of thick twine, at the end. I put my finger on it and follow it. It runs along the ground, under leaves, then through the dirt. My hand is dirty now, but I don't mind. This will lead me out of the labyrinth, maybe to Dionysus. It goes under a prickly brush, and I can't get through. Disappointed, I sit down. Darker. It is darker now. I should have brought a flashlight. The thin silver one I used to take camping with my family. I shiver in fear. Perhaps the minotaur is near. I crawl around the bush. My beige pants get caught in the prickles. When I pull out the prickles, I hear a rip. It doesn't matter. I probably won't wear these again. I feel around in the dark and finally find the thread again and follow it on my knees.

Darker. Darker and darker. My head hits something hard and I fall backwards into the bushes. I reach out my hand. Something cold. I push the brush away and some daylight creeps through. It is Theseus. I have found him. He is crouching. I look out and see the minotaur, not knowing that Theseus is near, but sniffing, possibly smelling him, knowing, does he know, will he pounce?

I whisper to Theseus. Shhhh. Be quiet. Don't make a sound. Just go get him! I touch the thread again. The other end is on his finger. I am pleased. We are still attached. Shhhh. Now kill him. Kill the monster.

The minotaur is moving, coming slowly toward us. Silently in the dark. I touch Theseus, try to warn him. He will win, though. He always wins. He will kill the monster, get the money, win the woman, leave her when she is sleeping. I was sleeping that last time, woke up to find him gone, gone with all the money. My job, my good name.

I must flee these monsters. I run blindly, up and down path after path, not thinking or choosing, I wish I could fly over these bushes and see the pattern. What is the pattern? A tree branch hits my face, I taste blood running down my cheek, into my mouth, I stumble and fall. I listen. Do I hear the soft footprints of the monster? Of Theseus? Where is the thread?

Crawling now again on hands and knees. I cannot see any pathways. There is no longer sky. My knees and palms are bleeding. I will never get out of here. Mother, where are you? I want to come home.

I look up. Red. Setting sun. Open sky. Stars. I crawl a little further and come out into a circle, a sacred place, with a statue in the centre. The god is here. So beautiful. More beautiful than Theseus. Gloriously naked. Broad smile. Eyes full of love. Radiating pleasure. Holding out to me a cup of wine. I lie at his feet, giggling. I reach for the cup.

The Birthday Gift

A PURSE, a woman's pocketbook, is locked in my aunt's coffin, buried underground, racing with her corpse towards dissolution. Which will decompose first, turn to ashes, dust? Like an ancient Egyptian, she has something with her, something that may perhaps be useful in her journey to the 'other side.'

It was my mother's idea, one dictated to her by a Greek custom she remembered learning from her mother or some other relative—or perhaps from her imagination. Her sister had died suddenly, one week before her fifty-fourth birthday. My mother had bought her a purse for her birthday, but had not had the chance to give it to her—one just like her own, an alligator-skin purse that Cal had admired.

After the initial shock of Cal's death was over and we sat quietly sobbing in my aunt's living room, my mother cried out, "Oh, no, oh, no."

"What is it?" I rushed to her, thinking that she had suddenly come out of numbness to realize that her sister had really died.

"The purse," she said, her voice trembling.

"What purse?"

"I bought Cal a purse for her birthday."

"Perhaps you can keep it for yourself."

"No, you don't understand. I bought her a gift that I didn't give her. Now she will come back from the dead to get me, to take me with her."

"Why would your own sister do that to you?"

"It's what the Greeks say. And it's true. Maybe she is jealous that she's dead and I'm still alive. Or maybe it's not really her who comes back, but an evil spirit, or devil, in her form. That spirit will come for me."

She continued sobbing, but then stopped. "I know what I'll do. I'll give her the purse now. Put it in her coffin with her."

"Do they let you do that?" I wondered, having already encountered several times the illogical regulations of our burial customs.

"I'll make them. Jerry will do it for me. I've known him for years."

Later, before leaving for the funeral home, she went to her bedroom and came back with a bag which apparently contained the purse. Her mouth was set tight with resolve, a resolve she displayed to Jerry the funeral director as soon as we arrived. I was angry at her. Her sister, my aunt, whom we had loved so deeply, and whom we would both miss desperately, was dead, we were about to see her dead body, a fact that frightened me since I did not want to believe she was dead and now would have to accept it—and my mother was arguing with the undertaker about placing a purse in the coffin, thinking more about her own feared death than about her sister's actual death.

As I had suspected, there was a regulation against it. But Jerry finally said, "I'll look the other way and you sneak it in—but hide it so I don't see it." My mother did just that, tucking the alligator-skin purse under the pink satin lining of the coffin just under Cal's feet, where the satin bunched out and could be used to cover any unsightly body parts that could not be made beautiful by the undertaker.

She waited until just before the funeral, when the coffin would be sealed forever. I almost giggled watching her surreptitious way of leaning over Cal's feet, lifting one foot a little, hiding the purse—she moved like a thief, stealing from someone who was just sleeping, who was likely to sit up any minute and say "Gotcha." I expected Cal to do just that—she and I could have had such a laugh over my mother's actions. Cal was always childlike and fun-loving. Her mother would scream, "Calliope, grow up, dress like a grown woman, behave yourself," but Cal would not grow up, and she and I were like best friends rather than aunt and niece.

Throughout the wake and the funeral, I thought of that purse. It helped me get through the grief, provided 'comic relief.' It certainly appeased my mother. She now could concentrate on her grief and forget her fear. Now her sister's ghost would not come to her one night, reach out a bony hand, and demand, "Come."

That night, after the funeral, I was sound asleep, dreaming that Cal and I were dancing the cha-cha on the beach, when my mother shook me, yelling loudly in my ear. I couldn't understand her—she was screaming and crying.

"Mom, what is the matter!" I wondered if someone else had died or was sick.

"Something terrible has happened!" She was crying so hard that I couldn't understand her for quite awhile. "I ... I ... put my own purse in the coffin instead of the one I bought for Cal. All my credit cards are in it, my licence, and some money."

"How did you manage to do that?"

"I was so nervous. And I left my purse, I thought it was my purse, at home, and just took my keys and some Kleenexes in my small purse. Instead of grabbing up Cal's purse, I must have grabbed my own. I don't know how I did it. Then tonight I opened my purse to look at Cal's picture that I keep in my wallet—I couldn't sleep, I missed her so—and I found the purse empty. Cal's purse! And my own purse is down in a hole in the ground with a dead body!"

I thought of the sealed coffin in the grave. "Maybe they haven't buried the coffin yet. We could have them open it, and you could switch purses."

"No, No. Don't you realize what that would mean? To take back a gift I had given her? Not to mention the sacrilege of opening the coffin after the funeral. She would come for me for sure. I would die violently because of my sin against her."

I had always wanted a sister, but now was glad I'd never had one. Was this an example of a relationship between sisters? This threat, this fear, this desire for each other's belongings and circumstances, this insistence on sharing every condition, even death?

I was awake now, but not enough to think clearly. "Let's make some coffee," I insisted, and stumbled out of bed to lead my mother to the kitchen. I started the coffee and tried to think of a logical way to solve this dilemma.

"Will Cal be angry at the gift you did give her, your own purse with all that's in it? Isn't that a good gift? She won't come for you then, will she?" Of course I wanted to tell her that this was all hogwash, but I didn't bother —she never listened to me.

"But what about my identification and credit cards?"

"You can get new ones quite quickly. I'll make the calls for you in the morning. We'll just say you lost your purse. Then, you can cancel those cards—not that Cal can use your credit cards, but we can't tell anyone where the purse is."

"You never know. Cal always envied me my credit cards."

"She did not. Mom, what's the matter with you?"

She began to cry again and I wished I hadn't said anything. But I was getting into her way of thinking now. "You know, since all your identification is in the coffin, and not Cal's, maybe someone will think that's your body and never come for you. You can live forever."

Her eyes brightened, then dulled. "I don't want to live

forever. But I want to live out my time and do more with my life. All I've done is be a mother."

I swallowed the clichés that almost came out and which perhaps she wanted to hear. She spoke again, though, rather quickly. "Yes, you're probably right, she won't come get me now, she'll appreciate the gift of my own purse and identification. I hope she doesn't mind —*she* knows who she is, anyway."

She started to walk out of the room. "Where are you going?"

"To bed. I'm tired." So she went to bed, and I sat up and drank coffee until morning, making a list of the phone calls I needed to make to get her new credit cards and a new license. I hoped she wouldn't tell anyone else about this, even my brother, who would just groan. I would not tell him. Let him go back to his home and his job without hearing of this dark side which he never liked to face.

I didn't tell any of my friends at university about this, not for a long time, though I wondered if this really was a Greek belief and why it had developed. I was studying anthropology and ancient religions and occasionally looked for such a superstition, found many similar ones, but nothing quite like that. I didn't try very hard, though. My friends would have laughed at my mother, at my heritage, if I had told them.

After Jack asked me to marry him, and I said yes, and we were in bed after beautifully happy lovemaking, and he had told me about his childhood fears, I told him the story of the purse. He listened quietly until I finished. Then he said, "God, your family's crazy. Are our children going to be that way?"

"Crazy! My family isn't crazy! My mother grew up with those beliefs. She inherited them."

"Then your family's been crazy for a long time."

"Are you implying that I'm crazy, too?"

"No, of course not. You must not have inherited that gene."

"Get out," I said.

"What?"

"Get out. I will not have anyone making fun of my mother and my family."

"But after what you told me, what do you expect? I'm not making fun of *you*."

"But I'm a product of that family. That Greek family. Perhaps you're prejudiced against Greeks. You're such a WASP. You WASPS have no imagination at all."

"Why are you so angry?"

"You could have tried to understand my mother, her suffering, her fear. Instead of saying she's crazy."

"Okay, don't get so excited. I thought *you* thought it was a strange and funny story."

I realized I had, until he'd said so. Now I had to defend my heritage.

"I guess you don't want to marry me now," I yelled.

"I didn't say that."

"You did. You said you didn't want to have children by me, in case they inherited the craziness."

"That's not exactly what I said."

"Get out."

He got dressed, while I waited in the bathroom with the door locked. I heard the door slam when he left.

He called me after that, several times, but I always hung up on him. Finally, he gave up. I *was* crazy to think I could marry a WASP.

After that, I told all my boyfriends, at least the ones I was serious about, the story of the purse. I wanted to see their reactions, use that to determine whether I'd be happy with them. My boyfriend from Ghana was furious at me for not using a certain spell that his grandmother had taught him to prevent the dead from coming back —but I told him over and over again that I did not know that spell. My Chinese boyfriend told me it didn't matter, not to take it seriously, not to worry. But most of them just laughed, thinking it a big joke, a funny story, only a story. I had one Greek boyfriend who didn't laugh but hadn't heard of that particular superstition—he said his family wasn't superstitious at all. He was sympathetic, though, since he found his family strange and rather primitive and never went to visit them.

My mother and I talked frequently on the telephone, but rarely about Cal. I reminded her one day about the purse, that our solution had worked, that Cal had never come back, that my mother's life had been healthy and happy, for, in fact, she was in love and about to marry again (something that hadn't happened to me!).

"Oh, Cal did come back," she said, "but just once."

"What?" I should have listened to Jack, I thought, she is crazy.

"Yes, she came back. But I explained to her about the mix-up and my decision to let her have my purse and all my credit cards and identification—told her I had really wanted to give her her birthday present—and she understood. She's stayed away since then."

Six months after her wedding and short honeymoon with her new husband, my mother had a stroke. I drove six hours to be with her and sat at her bedside as she slept. She had lost feeling in her left arm and left leg, and her speech was slurred. When she saw me there, she was not surprised. "Let me die," she said. "I want to die."

"C'mon, Mom. The doctor told me you'll pull through and might get all feeling back. You just need to work at it."

"I don't want to. I want to die."

I was always helpless against her words. She never listened to me. My words were useless, hitting the wall of her mind and bouncing back at me. So I was quiet. Then she mumbled something, and I leaned forward to hear her.

"It's because of the purse," she said.

"The purse?"

"Yes, my purse in Cal's grave, while I had hers. I never used it. Do you hear me, Cal, I never used your purse. I kept it, but it's yours. I bought a new one. And I gave you mine."

"But you said Cal came to you, that she understood."

"I never told you that. Why do you lie to me?"

"Mom, stop it, you did, you did tell me that."

"But now Cal is waiting for me," she continued, as

if I'd never spoken. "She will come for me. Come for me, Cal, you're right, I was selfish, I did all the wrong things, I was a bad sister, a bad mother, my children loved you more than they loved me. But I did try, I tried to give you your purse, for your very own."

All I could say was, "It's not true," over and over again, and "You tried to give her your purse, she'd never be mad," but she wasn't listening. After a while, her speech became too garbled for me to understand, and she went back to sleep.

Mike, my stepfather, came in, looked at her and sighed. "Is it my fault?" he asked sadly.

"Your fault? Now don't you start! How could it be? You've made her happy."

"I hope so. But why won't she fight?"

She woke up again, saw Mike, and smiled.

"Why won't you fight?" he asked her.

"Because my sister died first, and she was younger. It should have been me."

"Well, that's not the way things work all the time," Mike said. "It's not your fault she died first. But you're here. So hang on to life and get the most out of it."

Clichés, but she liked them. My mother always loved clichés, but I could never speak them. And Mike meant them. I might have meant them, too, but she wouldn't have believed me. So I kept silent. As did my brother. In this way we understood each other. He wandered around the hospital, saying nothing, like a shadow, like one of those zombies, unable to speak or to interrupt the flow of my mother's words, slurred and garbled, but constant and overwhelming. After a few days, he left, and so did I.

The next time I saw my mother she was in a wheelchair. The time after that she was walking with a cane. Mike was standing beside her, helping her when she needed or wanted to be helped. She was talking constantly. I tried to tell her about my studies, about my new apartment, but I couldn't explain what my life was like, so mundane and undramatic. She was talking about the male nurse who spoke Greek to her and made her move her arm. "He had a crush on me. He called me the Greek goddess." She talked about all the dead ones—her parents, her brothers, her sister, her first two husbands. I couldn't tell her about my boyfriends or my research into superstition, its harmful and beneficial effects on people who needed those beliefs to help them understand life and death. We talked about television shows and the movies she'd watched on her new VCR.

"I have a present for you," she said and reached for her purse, opened it and took out some money. "I have some money for you. Use it for something special for yourself. I gave your brother the same amount, so he won't be jealous." I didn't see the money or count how much it was—I was noticing the purse, made of alligator skin.

She saw me looking. "You know, I found this in the closet. Perfectly good. Never used. I must have forgotten about it. What a waste. So I'm putting it to good use now."

I folded up the money and put it in my purse—a black one made of fake leather. I was against killing alligators for their skin. "Thank you," I said. But she was already talking about something else, about somebody she'd seen on Oprah, about Mike's daughter who reminded her of me because she wrote poetry and published it in the newspapers, about how wonderful Elizabeth Taylor looked.

Unfinished

THE STREET LOOKED familiar, though Margo didn't remember walking here before. Used books, antiques, jewellery, pottery, paintings, hand-woven shawls. She looked in the window at the shawls, admiring the bright blue one and the cream one with tassels. Her reflection and the sun partly blocked her view of a third shawl, which seemed to have roses and violets on it. Too gaudy for her. She preferred something simple and plain. She was tempted to try the blue one on but walked past the shop.

Every day she walked in a different direction, as she learned her way around the city. She had moved here just two months ago. She had retired now, her husband had died one year ago, and she had been fortunate to find a small house just a few blocks from her older daughter's house and six blocks from her younger daughter's. Now she could spend more time with her grandchildren—or at least she had thought so. The families were so busy with work and school that she'd hardly seen them at all; she often walked by their houses only to find that no one was there.

A store called *Memories* advertised "Collectibles." Displayed in the window were teacups, napkin holders, antique picture frames, record albums, necklaces, bracelets, and animal figurines. Margo went in to browse. Maybe she could find some small gifts for the children. Ashleigh loved tiny dolls, Barry collected models of vintage cars, and baby Ryan enjoyed stuffed animals and soft books.

She didn't see anything for children. The attractive woman at the counter seemed friendly, though. She was probably in her sixties, a little younger than Margo. Her dark hair, speckled with grey, was pulled back in a bun and her long flowered dress rather old-fashioned. Her eyes and soft voice were kind; Margo wondered if they could become friends.

The woman smiled at Margo and said, "Welcome."

"Thank you," Margo said. "Do you have anything for children?"

"I'm sorry, not right now."

"I'll just browse, then, if you don't mind."

The woman nodded, and Margo wandered around the store: sets of china, silverware, used books, and, in the back, sheet music from the 1930s and 40s. Those were her mother's favourite songs, and hers. She used to play them on the piano, the spinet her mother had given her when she'd moved away for her first job. Now the piano was standing forgotten in her new living room. It hadn't been tuned in years. She wasn't sure if she could play anymore with her arthritic hands.

She leafed through stacks of music: "I Don't Want

to Set the World on Fire (I Just Want to Start a Flame in Your Heart)"; "Stardust"; "The Man I Love"; "I'll Be Seeing You." These were the songs she had loved and even used to sing with her mother. "It Had To Be You"; "Sentimental Journey." She took a stack of these to the front and got out her wallet.

"These are wonderful old songs," the woman said. "You'll enjoy playing them."

"Well, I haven't played in years. I don't even know if I can. But it will be something to do."

The woman paused and looked at her.

Margo explained. "I've just retired and moved here, so I'm looking for new hobbies."

"Do you live alone?"

"Yes, my husband died last year. But my two daughters live here with their families. I have three grandchildren. I moved here to see them more often—though I don't see them as often as I had hoped."

The woman slipped the sheet music into a bag for her. "You are so lucky. My children moved out west so I hardly ever see them."

"I'm sorry. That must be tough. Well, I better be on my way." Margo hated to leave. She'd been so lonely in her new home, and it was nice to talk to someone. "I'm Margo," she said. "What is your name?"

"Hi, Margo. I'm Anastasia but everyone calls me Anna. Stop by here anytime. By the way, there's a concert down in the park—chamber music, if you like that sort of thing. They are excellent musicians."

"Oh? Where is the park?"

"When you go out the door, head left, walk two blocks, and you'll see it on your right."

"Thank you so much. I think I'll do that."

Margo put the package into her shoulder bag and walked out into the sunlight. It was turning into a nice day, warmer than it had been in weeks. Spring was finally here. She found the park and headed toward the centre of it, where a crowd was gathering and musicians were setting up on a stage surrounded by a concrete divider. It looked like a spot for a fountain—but instead of a fountain there was a slightly raised platform. There were chairs available but they weren't set into rows—people were grabbing them and placing them wherever they wanted to sit. Some younger couples with children spread out blankets on the grass. Mothers were pushing babies in strollers and finding places to position them. Some older people, and some younger Asian people, had brought umbrellas to protect them from the sun. The musicians were tuning up, getting ready to start.

Margo looked around for a chair but couldn't find one. All chairs were occupied, some pulled up close to the concrete divider—but there was room to sit right on the divider. Margo did just that and put her feet in front, on the ground. The music was lovely—violin, viola, cello, keyboard—she didn't know much about classical music but this was pleasant and relaxing.

After the first piece was finished, Margo turned to the young man behind her. "I hope I'm not in your way," she said. He glowered at her. "Yes, you are," he said. "I wish you'd move." His voice had a slight accent that she couldn't place. "I'm sorry," she said, too shocked to argue with him. She swung her legs back over the divider and walked away. His rudeness had deeply upset her. She had been a university professor for thirty years and was not used to such treatment. She had been respected. Students had held doors open for her and offered to carry her books. Her face was burning and she thought she might cry.

She walked to further sections of the park, just wandering, looking for buds peeking through the ground, touching the barks of trees. The sun was so warm that she took off her sweater. She thought of sitting in the sun but had not brought her suntan lotion. She looked longingly at a rosy-cheeked baby resting contentedly in his stroller, remembering the times when she had pushed her children, and later her grandchildren, through parks.

The chamber group started to play something unusual, something so haunting that it drew her closer. She stood close to the divider, ignoring the rude man who had rebuked her earlier. This was the most beautiful music she had ever heard—light, mellow, haunting, joyful. Strings and piano—and singing. She hadn't realized that there was a small choir, as well as the musicians. They must have come later, while she was walking around the park. The voices and strings blended so beautifully, counterpointing, coming together, lifting her up; she forgot that she was standing there in a small park, alone.

Tears in her eyes. Warm arms lifting her up to the sky. Love in someone's eyes when looking at her. A feeling in the heart. Soft ... wings ... air ... birds ... sunlight ...

weightlessness. She could almost see the fountain that used to be there, hear the water spraying, see it sparkling.

Then the music stopped. So suddenly. So jarringly. The sun must be setting—the world seemed so dark and cold. She pulled her sweater around her. The fountain was gone; there was only concrete.

The music had stopped so abruptly—yet the piece did not seem finished. The performers were talking amongst themselves. She longed for them to keep playing and singing.

"Why did they stop?" she asked an elderly gentleman standing behind her.

"That piece is unfinished. Even the title was ripped from the manuscript that was found." His mouth curved downward. "I keep wishing they'd find the missing pages."

Margo didn't leave but continued standing there, even though the musicians and singers were packing up and the crowd had dispersed. She jumped when someone spoke to her. "Madam." It was the rude young man. "I am sorry for my rudeness. You like this music?"

"I love it," she answered, putting her hand up to shade her eyes so that she could see him. He was tall and slim, with dark hair. "But I didn't want it to end."

"Here." He handed her something, some papers bundled together. "This is the music, a gift for you, since you appreciated this so much."

She hesitated but took the bundle and looked at it. Music—for piano. Complicated. She'd never be able to play this.

"Thank you so much, but this is too difficult for me," she told him. But when she looked up, he was gone.

She put the music into her bag and started to walk home. She could not understand why the mysterious man had given this to her.

As she approached *Memories*, she decided to thank Anna for telling her about the concert. The music was still playing in her head. Anna looked up when she entered, smiling.

"Did you forget something? Was your sheet music all right?"

"Oh, yes. I just wanted to thank you for recommending the concert. It was wonderful!"

"Aren't they good? Did they play that amazing unfinished piece?"

"Yes, I found it haunting and joyful. I loved it!"

"You know, there's an urban myth about that. They say that if someone really appreciates the music, the composer (who has been dead for centuries) will come back and give that person a copy of the complete work, along with its title, for whatever instrument the person plays. The person will be able to play the piece but will never remember the title and will never tell anyone about it."

Margo had been going to tell her about the young man but then found that she couldn't. She thanked her, waved goodbye, and left.

When she got home, she took out the completed composition and looked at the title. She thought that she would always remember it. She sat down at her piano, spread it out before her, and started to play. She played it from beginning to end, over and over, so beautifully and perfectly. When she put the sheets of music away, she could not remember the title, until she looked at it again. Then she thought that she'd always known it and would never forget it. This was music that was always unfinished and always complete, unfinishing itself when she stopped, completing itself every time she played. Every time she played it, it was all new.

The Invention of Pantyhose:
An Autobiography

WALKING UP THIRD Avenue almost all the way to work then turning left and crossing avenues until I get to Fifth. I work in a travel agency now, though I used to work at *Look* magazine—couldn't get past the position of a secretary who was expected to plan men's dirty weekends and lie to their wives. I was fired because I wouldn't let my boss touch me. Now in my new job dirty men try to seduce me right in the office or lure me to a lunch that turns out to be an attempted rape. Men whistle when I walk down the street. What's wrong with me? I'm not that gorgeous. Look at all the models and movie stars who walk down those same streets. Don't pick on me. I'm happier in the Village, go to hear Allen Ginsberg read, everyone is hoping he'll say dirty words now that the new law was passed allowing more freedom of speech in public. But he doesn't. I waitress part time in a Middle Eastern restaurant but am accosted whenever I try to catch a taxi home by men who want me to go to their rooms with them and smoke pot. All I want is to be a writer.

The day I turn ten my best friend and I climb to the top of the trestle and stand next to the railroad track while the train goes by, making our hair stand on end and almost knocking us off the bridge. The sharp whistle pierces my eardrums and sends chills through my body. I'm so proud I did this! Summers are so long and hot, so wonderful—climbing the hills and exploring the woods, jumping across the creek on trails of rocks. Sometimes I fall in and come home soaking wet. Every morning I wake up with pleasure. I step into shorts and a tanktop —different colours every day—dash down to breakfast, and slam out the screen door for another adventure. We play kick the can until it is so dark we can't see the can. We play badminton in the dark, even though we can't see the birdie.

Someone throws a cat into my bed in the dormitory while I'm sleeping, a stray cat with a crooked head, scary-looking as hell. I wake up screaming and fear cats ever after. The girls two years behind me follow me everywhere singing, "All day, all night, Marianne," and unwrap my wrap-around skirt. I don't know what I'll do after graduation. Prostitute and nun are both on the list I make as I sit on my bed. Graduate school? Working in New York? Marriage?

The first year I don't get a doll for Christmas, I am devastated, trying not to cry. I look through all the packages. Something must be missing. I ask my mother, "Where is my doll?"

"We thought you were too old for a doll," she says.

My first baby is born one month early after I spent

two months in bed, bleeding. I hear a strange mechanical sound, then realize it is my baby crying. Is it a boy or a girl? I ask. A girl. Is she okay? Yes, she is fine. She is so tiny and doesn't know how to eat. Nurses bring her to me at all hours, and we try. Finally, she gets it.

I dance with my cousins on the dirt path between houses. We have oil lamps to help us see. This Greek village does not have electricity or plumbing. At night, I get up from my mattress on the roof and climb down to the toilet in the small shed. The mosquitos drive me crazy. I am covered with large lumps. I stay with cousins who keep a goat in the yard, between the house and the outhouse. I have to get by him in the dark. I wait until he moves away and run past. He is tied with a rope but the rope is long enough for him to reach me. I finish, wipe with newspaper clippings on a hook, and dash back before the goat can butt me.

The doctor holds up my granddaughter. She seems so big. Was she really inside my daughter? My daughter and I look at each other and weep with pleasure and relief. My son-in-law doesn't want to cut the cord, so I do, and blood spurts out. I scream. The doctor says this means good luck.

I am walking down Fifth Avenue on my way home when I realize that I can't see the street signs, it is getting darker and darker. Shadowy forms around me, murmurs, nervous questioning voices. I pass the Chrysler building but it is only a large shadow, no lights. I find my apartment building and people with flashlights lead me up the stairs. Major blackout. People think it is the Communists or some kind of attack. We cook packaged Rice-A-Roni on our gas stove but can't tell in the candlelight when it is browned. Some friends who can't get out of the city sleep on our floor. Even the phones don't work. We huddle in the darkness, frightened. My mother finally reaches me by phone. The blackout is there, too, all across the Eastern seaboard. We are terrified. Finally, I sleep, and wake up in the morning to blazing lights and the hum of power lines.

My mother and stepfather come to my graduation when I get my Ph.D. My husband already has his Ph.D.; he is there with our two daughters. We have a party. My mother dances the tango with one of the professors—they fly across the living room floor.

My grandparents come to bring me home from university at the end of my first year. I don't know why my parents don't drive down. We arrive home and my father comes out to carry my suitcases and boxes in. That night I hear him screaming in the night, horrible, horrible screaming. The ambulance comes, but he is too big for them to carry down the winding stairs on the stretcher. He sits on the stairway and lowers himself down, one step at a time. Later, a call comes from the hospital. My mother runs to her car, and I jump into the passenger seat. She tells me to stay home, but I won't. We get to the hospital, take the elevator, run to his room. The door is closed. "He is gone," we are told, and I start screaming.

Two brothers own the Syrian restaurant in the Village. Both of them want to sleep with me. They call me "the god-damn Greek." But I know they like me. They throw out any man who accosts me and help me get taxis safely. They also cook me dinner, whatever I want, when I arrive at work. The other waitresses stare at me in resentment. I am working at the restaurant on my birthday, depressed that no one is celebrating it with me, no one is saying happy birthday. A customer comes back with flowers. "I forgot to tip you," he says. I am so pleased. "It's my birthday," I tell him. Then, after work, one of the brothers pulls out a cake for me, and they all sing.

I dream of a chained up giant who gets free. The chain hangs loose in my kitchen, no giant attached. I am afraid. I dream of children uncared for. I must rush back to be sure that they are not alone. I have to take care of the children.

Snowfall. I ride to work with a friend. My husband, whom I married in Greece, drives in himself—he just got his license. He passes the school bus and collides with a tractor-trailer. I am left with a thirteen-month-old daughter. I dreamed it before it happened.

Every day after dinner I ride my bicycle around the neighbourhood. It is so quiet in this little town. In the winter, I dig tunnels in the snow and slide on the ice. At school we have roller skating parties and sock hops. I am the first to wear coloured tights under my skirts. Soon everyone is wearing them.

Pantyhose. No seams, no leg-digging garters, no tops of legs showing. One of the best inventions in the history of women. I babysit for the children of my girlfriend's new lover. She pays me in pantyhose.

The boy next door calls me "fat legs Harry," and I never forget it. I always cover my legs now.

My three grandchildren sit on my lap, smiling; I put this picture on Facebook.

I really wanted a doll for Christmas.

Another daughter. She kisses her dolls, her toys, but not us, not for a long time. I tell her not to be afraid, the goddess Diana is in the moon and will protect her. She says, "Mom, the moon is the moon."

Newgrange in Ireland, Tim and I crawl inside the 5000-year-old structure, stand inside the circular centre, imagining the winter solstice, light running along the pathway, curving its way to fulfilment, to endless cycles. The light always returns.

I sit in my playpen and wail. "Howlagellup?" Someone comes and stands me up. I clutch the side and wail again. "Howlagetdown?"

Crossing the bridge over the creek, kissing my boyfriend on the bridge, the neighbours complain, my mother scolds me, but he and I walk at dusk, hand in hand.

My grandfather calls me "Blotso." "What does that mean," I ask him. "That's Greek for good looking," he says.

A girl in the Greek village notices my pantyhose as we climb up the hill. She has never seen anything like them. "How can your stockings go all the way to the top?" she asks. After I return to America, I send her a pair. She saves them for special occasions. I don't remember this but she never forgot that gift. She tells me this as we sit in her stuffy, darkened apartment in a suburb of Athens. Her thirty-six-year-old daughter died of cancer five months earlier. We look at her photograph on the wall. We talk about pantyhose.

I ride my bicycle all around town every summer night after dinner. Then we play kick the can until the darkness turns the can into an invisible shadow. We go home for popcorn and juice and television. I sleep peacefully in my bedroom with its yellow-flowered wallpaper and golden curtains. A weeping willow tree caresses the window and protects me from harm. Can't wait until morning.

Acknowledgements

Three of these stories were published in issues of *Event* magazine: "No Man" (as "No Man's Castle"); "The Sacrifice"; and "Thirteen" (as "Trinities"). I wish to thank my husband, J.R. (Tim) Struthers, for reading these stories and giving me such good advice; my nephew Ioakim Kountalis and my cousin Yiannis Mikrogiannakis for answering my questions about Greek names; and the University of Guelph for granting me a research leave that gave me the time to write and revise many of these stories.

About the Author

Marianne Micros, in her story collection *Eye* and other writings, explores the mythology, folklore, Greek customs, and old-world cultures that have fascinated her all her life. Her previous publications include: a book of poetry about her Greek family (*Upstairs Over the Ice Cream*, Ergo); a poetry collection that focuses primarily on her search for ancestors and family members in Greece (*Seventeen Trees*, Guernica); and poems and short fiction in anthologies and journals. She has also published scholarly articles on Renaissance and contemporary subjects and a bibliographical monograph on Al Purdy. Marianne's suite of poems *Demeter's Daughters* was shortlisted for the Gwendolyn MacEwen poetry competition in 2015 and published in *Exile: The Literary Quarterly*. Marianne obtained her Ph.D. in English from The University of Western Ontario and, after some thirty years of teaching, has now retired from her career as an English professor at the University of Guelph, where she taught Renaissance literature, Scottish literature, folktales, and creative writing. Marianne is currently compiling her new poems into a book entitled *The Aphrodite Suite* and is working on a second collection of stories.